Eagle Nebula

Lionel Ray Craft

DORRANCE PUBLISHING CO
EST. 1920
PITTSBURGH, PENNSYLVANIA 15238

Dorrance Publishing Co
585 Alpha Drive
Pittsburgh, PA 15238
Visit our website at *www.dorrancebookstore.com*

ISBN: 979-8-88812-209-9
eISBN: 979-8-88812-709-4

PREFACE

The Eagle Nebula is a young cluster of stars located in the constellation Serpens. This nebula is approximately 5,700 light years from Earth with an age estimated between one and two million years. In 1995, the Hubble Space Telescope photographed a region within the Eagle Nebula called "The Pillars of Creation." These structures, which resemble stalagmites in a cave, are believed to be the incubators for new stars as well as planets and brown dwarfs.

Beginning in 2035 and completed in 2038, the U.S. Government spent $2.8 billion to develop the most powerful and advanced computer in the world. This computer, called the Advanced Cosmological Theoretical Observational and Research (ACTOR) computer, had the ability to process mega amounts of data and provide the answers within a fraction of time of the best computers of its era. But what made ACTOR truly extraordinary was its ability to undertake deductive reasoning. After several years of operation, the President of the United States directed the scientists operating the computer to have the computer provide answers to three profound questions about life, the fate of the human race and the existence of God. The computer, the scientists who operate it and the computer's answers are the story of this novel.

CHAPTER ONE

The Advanced Cosmological Theoretical Observational Research (ACTOR) computer was located in a one-story building on the grounds of the Argonne National Laboratory, in Lemont, Illinois. During its inception, ACTOR was developed to increase our understanding of the atom and its components, as well as the Universe as a whole. All known scientific data associated with atomic energy, physics, astronomy and biochemistry were uploaded and processed by the computer. Shortly after ACTOR became fully operational, in 2040, it had profoundly enhanced our knowledge of our solar system as well as the Universe. ACTOR theorized that biochemical life would be found in the upper atmospheres of Jupiter and Saturn, as well as in the regions immediately beneath the atmospheres of Uranus and Neptune and on as well as below surface of Saturn's moon Titan. ACTOR ruled out places such as Mars, Jupiter's moon Europa and Saturn's moon Enceladus as abodes for biochemical life. Subsequent probes to Jupiter, Saturn and its moon Titan confirmed the existence of unique but microscopic forms of biochemical life. Moreover, after reviewing detailed photographic data of the Moon's surface, ACTOR indicated that a site within Mare Serenitatis would provide proof that intelligent, alien life existed and had landed on the Moon's surface in the past. A subsequent mission to the Moon in 2042 confirmed a site that initially was thought to be a small crater, but due to its perfect symmetry appeared to be the base and landing site used by an alien civilization. The site was lined with an exotic material that did not naturally exist on the Moon and the site's age was estimated at between 100,000 and 200,000 years old.

ACTOR discounted the "Big Bang Theory" and theorized, based on its astronomical data, that the star Cygnus X-1 (among others) was not being orbited by a stellar black hole, but a black dwarf star, which was not thought to exist at this point in the Universe's life. ACTOR also indicated that the Universe was comprised of both physical and metaphysical components. The latter of which are black holes, gravity and space-time.

Relative to the Big Bang Theory, ACTOR determined that the components that make up the Universe, such as the galaxies, stars and planets, have ages, but the Universe itself does not. ACTOR also indicated that because of the vast size of the observable Universe, the greater the distance from Earth, the Universe becomes more of an illusion and that phenomena such as space-time, dark energy and black holes were areas where the physical and metaphysical components of the Universe converge.

In addition to astronomy, ACTOR's research in nuclear physics provided information that led to the development of the world's first operational nuclear fusion reactor that was located nearby at the Fermi National Accelerator Laboratory (Fermilab) in Batavia, Illinois. Several fusion reactors were now operating or under construction throughout the U.S. and the world.

ACTOR was housed in a U-shaped, non-descript, one-story, beige brick building, with glass block windows, except at the entryway. One wing of the approximately 100,000 square foot building housed the computer and related components. The remainder of the structure contained a conference room, an administrative office, a kitchen/breakroom, a storage room and two bedrooms that were infrequently used by the staff. The building was not open to the public because some of the computer's projects were classified as "top secret." Consequently, the area surrounding the laboratory was fortified and heavily guarded. In the wing housing ACTOR, the massive computer sat on an elevated concrete platform in a wing that was higher than the rest of the building. This was to ensure ample air circulation for the computer and protect it from a flood.

The scientists and technicians assigned to ACTOR were Bruce Morrow, the Project Manager; Jessica Minton, the Assistant Project Manager Joseph Mkapa, Fazlur Pandit, Evelyn Dodge, Boris Krutov, Howard Stanton, and Lena Anderson. Anderson handled the administrative duties as well as cleaning the lab. Bruce grew up in Westfield, New Jersey, is age 62, single and twice divorced with no children. Bruce received a doctorate degree in astronomy from Harvard University, and prior to ACTOR, he was a professor at Stanford University. Jessica0, age 59, was a widow with an adopted daughter, who was born in China. Jessica, who grew up in Fresno, California, received a doctorate degree in bio-chemistry from the University of California, at Los Angeles. Joseph, age 41, was born in Tanzania, married with one child. Joseph earned a doctorate degree in chemistry from the Massachusetts Institute of Technology (MIT).

Fazlur, age 55, was born in India, where he received an undergraduate degree in biology from the University of Mumbai and a doctorate degree in physics from Oxford University in England. Fazlur (called Faz by his peers) was married with two adult children. Evelyn, age 37, was married, no children and earned a master's degree in computer science from Northwestern University and a doctorate degree in the same field, from the University of Chicago. Boris, age 45, was born in eastern Russia and came to the United States as part of a scientific exchange program. Boris earned his undergraduate and graduate degrees from Moscow State University, where he majored in cosmology. Boris was single, no children. Howard, age 40, is married with three children, received his undergraduate and graduate degrees in chemistry from the University of Michigan. Lena, age 29, was married with one child. Lena earned an MBA degree from Roosevelt University.

CHAPTER TWO

ACTOR was one of America's technological triumphs of the decade. Socially and economically, America was in a slow decline, as a result of political and social divisions and the shift from a manufacturing-based economy to a consumer economy wherein most goods were imported. China and India were now the world's manufacturing powerhouses. The federal government was also weakened by years of overspending as well as the enormous deficit. This deficit was exacerbated by global warming created droughts, forest fires, tornados, hurricanes and coastal flooding. Moreover, America's economy never recovered from the pandemic of the 2020s and the rise in violent crimes that affected every sector of the country. In response to the rising crime and tightening budgets, many towns were merging with adjacent towns to consolidate their police and fire departments, as well as their primary and secondary schools.

In 2040, over half of all vehicles were either hybrid or all electric as gas prices were approximately $10 a gallon. High energy costs, along with smaller and fewer nuclear families, made small homes more fashionable and desirable. The effects of global warming had reduced the size of the global icecaps by twenty-five percent over the last century. Consequently, millions of acres of the eastern seaboard were now submerged and dikes were erected around Miami and New York City (among others). Worldwide, the rising sea level resulted in mass relocations, increased poverty, diseases and loss of life.

As a result of the high cost of space exploration, the International Space Agency (ISA), comprised of the United States, Great Britain, France, Germany, Nigeria, South Africa, China, Russian, Brazil and Argentina, handled all space endeavors. ISA was constructing a permanent base on the Moon, while thoroughly investigating the aforementioned site in Mare Serenitatis. Although ACTOR was solely funded by the U.S. government, its astronomical research was shared with ISA.

On a Monday morning in April 2040, Bruce identified himself at the perimeter security gate before entering a small parking lot adjacent to the ACTOR lab. After punching the access code on an exterior monitor, Bruce peered into an optical receptacle wherein he was identified via the structure of his iris. Afterwards, the steel entrance door retracted and Bruce entered the building. Upon entering the main working area, motion detector lights brightened the interior. Bruce went to his office in the corner of the building, put away his charcoal gray wool coat, started his personal coffee maker and checked his emails. A few minutes later, Jessica entered the lab and over the next hour the remaining staff arrived.

At about 9 a.m., after everyone had settled in and checked their emails, Bruce called a meeting in the conference room to review and discuss ACTOR's response to data that was submitted the previous week. The response was associated with a question about two planets encircling a neutron star in the constellation Orion. Bruce summarized ACTOR's response:

"I hope you guys enjoyed you weekend because this is going to be a busy week. The scientific community has long wondered how planets could survive, let alone exist, in orbit around a neutron star. It was long believed that when a massive star left the main sequence and expelled its outer layers, any planets in this system would either be destroyed or ejected from the star's solar system. This is not the case, however, with Orion XG4, along with a few other neutron stars. Until recently, the nature of these planets had been a mystery. As you know, we asked ACTOR to analyze photographs and data from the James Webb Telescope, along with data from various gamma ray and infrared satellites. According to ACTOR, Orion XG4's planets were present throughout the star's history, but by the time the star grew into a red giant, it had slowly discarded a sizeable portion of its mass. This allowed the two planets to increase their orbits. The two planets, XG4a, which is slightly larger than earth and XG4b, which is about eight times larger than Earth, initially had orbits of 600 million and 1.2 billion miles, respectively. By the time XG4 expanded in size and expelled its outer layers, the planets' orbits had increased 28.436 percent. The two planets survived, in part, because of their distance from XG4 and the fact that they are quite dense, being composed primarily of iron, silicon and carbon. Consequently, XG4a and XG4b were singed after the star exploded, but survived. Some of XG4's debris, which was primarily gas and dust, remained in the system for a while, which slowed the orbits of the two planets, due to friction. This caused them to migrate inward, to their current orbits of 34 million and 97 million miles. ACTOR indicated that XG4a has an alloyed silicon-carbon crust, a crystalline carbon mantle and an iron core. XG4b is similar in structure but has an atmosphere comprised primarily of carbon monoxide with traces of carbon dioxide, argon and methane."

"That's quite interesting. I wonder if that's the case with the planetary systems of other neutron stars," Evelyn said.

"Who knows? That would be a separate question for ACTOR, who would first need all available data for the system in question. I'll tell you what, let's go to our modules where we can submit any follow-up questions to ACTOR," Bruce said.

Each member logged on until they were connected with ACTOR. Access to the computer was restricted to the lab because of the enormous safeguards employed to prevent hacking and computer viruses. ACTOR responded to questions with a synthesized male voice via the labs speaker system or emails.

"Hello, ACTOR, the group and I have follow-up questions related to your XG4 response. Based on the data in your memory banks, we would like to know if there are any similarities with the two planets orbiting XG4 and those orbiting neutron star PSR1257?" asked Bruce.

"*In response to your question, PSR1257 has three confirmed planets and at least one other planet that is suspected but has yet to be confirmed. Due to the star's distance, combined with our current data on this system, I am unable to provide any additional data beyond what we currently know,*" ACTOR responded.

"Thank you, ACTOR."

"I have a question for ACTOR," said Joe.

"Submit your question, Joe," Bruce said.

"ACTOR, based on some of the astronomical data you've recently examined, you've indicated that the three stars with unusual movements in the constellation Virgo, that have no visible companion stars, are being orbited by a black dwarf star. How can this be, when such objects are not yet thought to exist?"

"*As you are aware, most astronomers place the age of the Universe at approximately 13.8 billion years. Black dwarfs, which are white dwarf stars that no longer emit light or heat, are not believed to exist at this time, because of the belief that it would take a white dwarf over a trillion years to become a black dwarf star. I disagree with this theory because our concepts of age and time are incompatible with that of the Universe. The stars in question are binaries with an invisible companion. These companions have solar masses ranging from 1.2 to 2.7, which is consistent with the masses of white dwarfs. I suspect there are many black dwarfs in our galaxy as well as the Universe, but the current state of our technology is unable to substantiate this."*

"That's quite interesting. Thanks, ACTOR," Joe replied.

"Recently, ACTOR was processing all of our current data on the moon and I wonder if ACTOR has completed his theory on the Moon's formation. May I submit that question?" Faz asked.

"Sure. I think we all want to know what ACTOR's theory is," Bruce said.

After Faz submitted his question, ACTOR provided the following response:

"Unless we find a way to go back in time, we will never know how the Moon actually formed. However, based on the data I have processed, my conclusion is that the Moon did not form from debris as a result of early Earth's collision with another planet sized object, which currently is the most popular theory. My data suggests that the Earth and the Moon started forming concurrently from the proto-planetary disc surrounding our infant sun. The Earth was the larger globule in this region of the solar system and was able to attract and absorb the bulk of the gas and dust, in addition to a larger proportion of the heavier elements than the globule that formed the moon. The Earth/Moon globules initially orbited the Sun in tandem, with both revolving at about the same rate, with a seven-hour day. At some point, during the coalescing stage, the Moon slowly began to orbit the Earth. Tidal friction between the two slowed Earth's rotational speed and eventually

caused the Moon's rotation to stop, relative to the Earth. My problem with the collision theory is that if a planetary object with about the mass of Mars had collided with Earth, it would have greatly destabilized Earth's orbit, tilt and rotation. Moreover, this would have prevented the Earth from collecting water for its oceans in addition to developing its largely nitrogen-based atmosphere. Additionally, the Moon in its current state would not have formed from such a collision because the ejected material from the impact would have lacked the velocity required to escape Earth's Roche gravitational limit. If this were the case, this debris would be absorbed by the Earth."

"Thanks, ACTOR. Guys, let's take a half hour break and afterwards we will meet in the conference room. I have an announcement to make," Bruce said.

After the group was seated in the conference room, Bruce made the following announcement:

"Guys, next week, Jessica and I are attending the annual International Astronomical Conference, which is being held this year in Washington D.C. Director Hogan just informed me that immediately after the conference, President Ramsey wants to meet with Jessica and I at the White House. Hogan said he was not invited, which is not surprising since he was a compromise appointment by the president. I think it's unusual, however, that the president wants a meeting with us and I have no clue what this meeting is about," Bruce said.

"I think that's great. Maybe we'll get more funding or a hefty wage increase," said Evelyn.

"I doubt that, Evelyn, because they recently increased our funding and are unlikely to do so anytime soon," Faz responded.

"Does Hogan know what the meeting is about?" Howard asked.

"Hogan does not, but he suspects it pertains to either national security or the military," Bruce replied.

"If that's the case, isn't that a violation of ACTOR's intended purpose?" Boris asked.

"Look, I'm only speculating, so let's not get beyond ourselves. As you know, ACTOR's creation was brought about by President Ramsey and it is funded by the federal government to increase our understanding of the Universe. Such being the case, the government can authorize its use for non-scientific endeavors," Bruce said.

"Bruce, our next project is to provide ACTOR with data from our recent probe into the Oort Cloud. Should we proceed in your absence?" Evelyn asked.

"What do you think, Jessica?" Bruce asked.

"I think we should hold off until you and I return from Washington. That's just in case the president has something that takes priority," Jessica replied.

"That's a good idea. Guys, Jessica and I will meet you at 9 a.m. sharp in the conference room upon our return from Washington, next Wednesday," Bruce said.

CHAPTER THREE

Arch Ramsey was near the end of his second term as President of the United States. A former Governor of Iowa, Ramsey was 64, six feet one inches tall, with a medium girth and speckled gray hair. Ramsey was a widower with two grown children and a Democrat. Ramsey was married to his college sweetheart and soul mate, Lynn Ramsey, until her death from ovarian cancer near the end of his first term. During his youth, Ramsey sporadically attended church, since his parents considered themselves agnostics. Lynn Ramsey adopted the Methodist religion but infrequently attended church. Instead, Lynn focused on her spirituality and her relationship with God. Just weeks before her death, Lynn asked Arch if he would mind if she reached out to him from the spiritual world to let him know that she lived on, but in a different realm. Believing this was impossible, but not wanting to disappoint her, Arch replied: "Sure, Lynn."

About a year after Lynn's death, Arch was awakened one night from some movement in his bed, which was the same bed he had shared with Lynn. At first, he thought it was his imagination until the movement continued. At this point, Arch, who was lying on his back, extended his left arm to the side where there was movement. Upon doing so, Lynn grasped his hand and raised it. In the feeble light of the room, Arch could see the silhouette of Lynn's body and her arm held up his arm, as well as feeling her presence. Arch then shouted, "Lynn, oh Lynn!" feeling both disbelief and delight. Immediately afterwards, Arch reached over to hug Lynn, but upon doing so, she vanished.

Following this event, Arch shared what he described as a "profound super-natural experience" with his closest family and friends and it renewed his faith in God.

"I was informed by my staff to meet you at 2 p.m., in the Oval Office, Mr. President," said Vice President Milton Sorrell. Milton was born and raised in Houston, Texas, where he received his undergraduate and graduate degrees in political science from Rice University and his law degree from Penn State. Two years younger and a few inches shorter than Ramsey and sporting a shaved head and medium build with a moderate stomach bulge, Sorrell had no further political ambitions after Ramsey finished this term.

"Milton, in a few minutes we will be joined by the two most senior members of the ACTOR team. What we discuss here today is top secret and should not be shared with anyone outside this office, do you understand?"

"Yes, Sir Mr. President. ACTOR has done some great things in the field of science, nuclear physics and astronomy. The scientists assigned to ACTOR should be applauded for their work. Is this the reason of their visit?"

"Milt, I have less than two years left in office and this country is in need of a moral boost to counteract the violent crimes in this country. My hope is that the ACTOR computer can answer questions that have lingered since the beginning of humanity. "

"What questions are those, Mr. President?"

"There are several questions I would like the computer to answer."

"Mr. President, Bruce Morrow and Jessica Minton are here," the Chief of Staff announced.

"Bring them in ten minutes. Milt, I want ACTOR to answer three things. One, what is life and the likelihood of its existence elsewhere in the Universe. Two, what is the likely fate of the human race, and three, is there a God or supreme being."

"Those are some profound questions, Mr. President, but don't you think it unwise to use this computer to answer something that it was not developed for and to expect it to provide answers for something that's both mysterious and philosophical?"

"Milt, I respect your opinion, but throughout human history, God has been the greatest mystery, in addition to our reason for existing. Due to the mystery of God, many religions have been created with each offering their vision of God. In addition to the religions, we have many agnostics and who knows how many atheists. Wars have been and are still being fought over the idea of God. I'm hoping that ACTOR can provide an answer, which will hopefully give humanity a unified concept of God. Moreover, I believe in an afterlife and would like to know if ACTOR can confirm its existence."

"Mr. President, as amazing as ACTOR's achievements are, what if the computer cannot answer the question about God, or if it concludes that either God does not exist or that God is fundamentally different from what humans believe? Are you prepared to deal with the chaos and repercussions such answers might bring?"

"I am aware and that is why this will be a top-secret project, which will allow me to control the narrative. After we receive answers from ACTOR, I will decide if they are fit for public consumption. If they are not, all data associated with this mission will be destroyed." Without further discussion, Ramsey directed his Chief of Staff to bring Bruce and Jessica into the Oval Office.

After Bruce and Jessica were introduced, Ramsey revealed his plan for ACTOR and asked whether or not it was possible for the computer to answer the questions he proposed.

"It's unprecedented, Mr. President, but I think the computer may be able to provide answers to your questions if it is fed the appropriate data to make a decision. Bear in mind that ACTOR may only provide theoretical or hypothetical answers since there is no raw data to support a definitive answer. ACTOR has done some amazing things and what really makes the computer unique is its ability to perform deductive reasoning. Consequently, ACTOR may be able to answer the questions you propose about life, the fate of the human race and even the existence of God. Overall, this will be an enormous challenge for the computer, as well as for the scientists operating it," Bruce said.

"Well, I want your team to pursue this project as soon as possible and it will be your top priority. Moreover, this endeavor is considered top secret." I'm going to have the two of you sworn to secrecy and a member of my staff will meet with the remainder of your team when you return to Illinois. Do not discuss this project with anyone other than your fellow colleagues and especially not to Director Hogan. Do you understand?"

"Yes, Mr. President," Bruce and Jessica said, in unison.

"Any idea how long it will take to complete this project?" Ramsey asked.

"Nothing of this magnitude has ever been done before, but I'm guessing it will take a few months to feed the necessary data to ACTOR and maybe a few months afterwards to get all the answers. So, let's say about six months or so. Do you want to be informed after the answer to each question is provided?" asked Bruce.

"No, that won't be necessary, Mr. Morrow. Once the entire project is completed, we will meet here in the Oval Office. I appreciate you and Ms. Minton coming here today and if you need anything, please contact my Chief of Staff. By the way, this project will be called *Eagle Nebula,* understood?"

"Yes, Mr. President," Bruce and Jessica replied.

Shortly thereafter, Bruce and Jessica took an oath, administered by the president and signed a form associated with their oath.

"Any questions before you depart, Mr. Morrow?"

"No, Sir Mr. President."

"How about you, Ms. Minton?"

"Yes. I'm curious as to why you named this project Eagle Nebula?"

"You may not know this, but since childhood I've had an interest in astronomy and I keep abreast of developments in this field of study. It's also one of the reasons I promoted the funding and development for ACTOR. I chose Eagle Nebula because the eagle is a symbol of the United States and this nebula, which as you know, is located in the constellation Serpens, has a region called the Pillars of Creation, where stars are being born. Hopefully, the use of this name will dissuade outsiders from prying into the true nature of this project."

"Thank you, Mr. President," said Jessica.

Following their meeting at the White House, Bruce and Jessica returned to their hotel, via an executive limo. While enroute, they did not discuss their meeting with the president and vice president. After they were deposited at their hotel, Bruce said: "Jessica, before we retire for the evening, can we meet to discuss Eagle Nebula?"

"Most certainly, that's what I was thinking. I'll tell you what, first I'm going to take a shower, and since this project is so confidential, why don't you come to my room in an hour and we can discuss this privately. When you come, we can order something to eat through room service. By the way, I'm in room 1742."

"Sounds like a good idea. See you in an hour."

After checking his emails and changing into some comfortable attire, Bruce went to Jessica's room, which was on the same floor. When Jessica opened her door, Bruce hid his surprise upon seeing Jessica clad in a robe with her brown hair draping on her shoulders. This was the first time he saw her looking romantic and sexual. Bruce, however, made no comment about her appearance. After reviewing the menu and ordering their meals, the following conversation took place:

"I don't know about you, but I was completely surprised by the president's request," Jessica said.

"So was I. I was expecting a reward or something related to national security."

"Same here. I don't know about you, Bruce, but I have mixed feelings about this project. For one, it's not what ACTOR was conceived to do, and secondly, I'm not sure if I want to know the answers to the president's questions."

"I feel the same, but this is the president and ACTOR is owned and funded by the federal government, so like it or not, we have to comply with his request."

"How do you think our colleagues will feel? Most likely their feelings will be in line with ours. But whatever the case, it will be intriguing to hear what this brilliant computer divulges about God, life and the fate of humans."

"Maybe so, but are we ready for that? These questions are highly controversial and many of us will not like the answers."

"Perhaps so, but that is not our problem. Let's not lose sight of the fact that ACTOR is just a computer, albeit an extraordinarily smart computer, but nevertheless, a computer designed and constructed by humans. Therefore, ACTOR is not omniscient and it can only make deductions based on the data fed into it. "

"That's true, but I'm afraid that some people will accept ACTOR's responses as the final truth and that's scary."

"I won't deny that, but whatever ACTOR concludes, assuming it can reach a conclusion, it won't improve our lives, like the president hopes, but it will only add to the confusion and divisions that already exist."

"I totally agree. Bruce, I want you to forget that I'm subordinate to you for maybe an hour or so, as I will suppress the fact that you're my superior. Would you consider having sex with me? If you say no, I won't be offended and I'll completely understand."

"Jessica, you must've read my thoughts. I would be delighted to have sex with you as long as it doesn't compromise our working relationship. If you can agree on that, I'm all for it."

"I promise that won't happen and I'm not looking to start a relationship with you. My reason for asking is that I haven't had sex since I briefly dated a guy I met online, over a year ago."

"No need to explain. I was turned on the moment I saw you in that robe."

"That was my intent," Jessica said as they both laughed. "I'll tell you what, let's order something to eat first and afterwards we can spend the night together, if that's okay with you."

"That's fine with me."

The next day, Bruce and Jessica returned home, via a flight back to Chicago.

CHAPTER FOUR

Shortly after he settled in at his Batavia, Illinois townhouse, Bruce called the lab and asked Lena to inform the team that a mandatory meeting was scheduled for 9 a.m. the following morning. Afterwards, Bruce checked his messages and mail, showered and microwaved a meal. While eating, he reflected on the meeting at the White House and his unexpected tryst with Jessica. He wondered how these events would affect his work at the lab. Bruce's thoughts were soon interrupted by his telephone. The caller ID indicated the caller was the lab's director, Hogan.

"Hi, Director Hogan."

"Hi, Bruce. I was calling to see how your meeting went with the president."

"The meeting went well, Director."

"Unfortunately, I wasn't invited, so you will have to fill me in on what was discussed."

"The president commended our team on ACTOR's accomplishments, but he gave us an unusual assignment. Unfortunately, this assignment is top secret so I'm not at liberty to discuss it with you."

"Bruce, as your boss and as the Director of ACTOR, I'm commanding you to at least give me the nature of your assignment."

"I'm sorry, Director, but that is a matter you will have to clear with the president. Jessica and I had to take an oral and written oath for total secrecy and the rest of the team will do so tomorrow. Why the president wants to keep you in the dark is between you and the president, so it's a waste of time for you to pressure me or the team about this assignment."

"I understand, Bruce, and I apologize. I will try to find out from other sources and if there's anything I can do to help facilitate your assignment, don't hesitate to call me."

"Thanks, Director, I appreciate that."

After the call, Bruce was sure that Director Hogan would continue to pry until he found out the nature of their project. Hogan was a power hungry, persistent and aggressive individual with political aspirations. Hogan was formerly a computer engineer and the founder of Compucorp, ACTOR's manufacturer. Hogan, however, was a member of the opposition party who always supported the president's opponents. Hogan was selected by President Ramsey to oversee the ACTOR program as a result of his role in developing the computer, but nothing more.

Just before retiring for the evening, Bruce thought a little about Hogan and Jessica, but especially the Eagle Nebula project. Bruce re-examined his religious beliefs as well as his belief in God. Born and raised in Westfield, New Jersey, Bruce was the middle son (an older sister and a younger brother) of an upper middle-class family. His father was employed as a civil engineer and his mother was a professor at Rutgers University. Bruce's parents were religious, and until he went off to college, he was required to regularly attend a nondenominational church nearby. Consequently, Bruce embraced the Protestant religion's belief that God was the creator of the Universe and that God's only begotten son, Jesus Christ, had died for our sins. By the time Bruce graduated from Harvard, he had modified his beliefs and now considered God to be an existential entity, with little or no involvement in human affairs. Bruce wondered if Eagle Nebula would change, reinforce or annihilate his beliefs.

Bruce met and married his first wife, Margaret Acevedo, shortly after he became an astronomer at the Las Campanas Observatory in La Serena, Chile. Bruce was twenty-eight at the time and Margaret, age twenty-five, was the daughter of a senior astronomer. Two years into their marriage, Margaret suffered a miscarriage at a time when Bruce had become weary of life in Chile. Bruce applied for and was offered a professorship at Stanford University. Their marriage ended when Margaret declined to relocate with Bruce to the United States.

Sherice Cohen was forty-six and Bruce fifty-one on the date of their marriage in California. Sherice was Jewish, but indifferent about religion and overall, an agnostic. Bruce met Sherice at a friend's party, and other than their love of travelling, both had clashing, Type A personalities. Their marriage lasted less than four years. Bruce, who was five feet ten inches tall, medium build, and who sported a mustache, along with a shaved head, now dedicated his life to astronomy and preferred to sidestep committed relationships. He hoped that Jessica felt the same way.

Shortly after entering her two-bedroom condo in Geneva, Illinois, Jessica first attended to her cat and then checked to see if she had received any messages from her daughter, Shensi. Shensi, who was named after the China province where she was born, was adopted by Jessica and her deceased husband. Shensi, now twenty-three, recently went to China to locate and hopefully meet her natural parents. Jessica was growing concerned because she had not heard from Shensi in almost a week, which was highly unusual.

After settling in, Jessica called her sister Betsy, who lived in Bakersfield, California, to find out if Betsy or her daughter Carol (Jessica's niece) had heard from Shensi, since they communicated regularly. Jessica also wanted to tell Betsy about her visit with the president. Neither Betsy nor Carol had heard from Shensi. Shortly thereafter, Jessica received a call from Hogan:

"Hi, Director. You've never called me on my home phone, so what's up?"

"Hi, Jessica. I was just calling to see how your meeting with the president went?"

"It went well and he expressed an appreciation for our work and success."

"I understand he made a special request. Can you talk about it?"

"I'm afraid not, because the project is top secret."

"You can't discuss it with your boss?"

"No disrespect, sir, but the president is everyone's boss."

"I can't argue with that. Anyway, welcome back, and if you or your coworkers need anything from me, don't hesitate to call."

"Thanks, Director."

Following the call, Jessica reflected on the meeting at the White House, which was a career highlight and her evening with Bruce. She had always admired Bruce and having sex with him was icing on the cake. Jessica, however, decided that she would not pursue a committed relationship nor a friend-with-benefits relationship with Bruce. Jessica considered their encounter to be a one and done event and hoped that Bruce felt the same way.

Next her thoughts drifted to the Eagle Nebula project. Up to this point, Jessica had come to believe that ACTOR was nearly infallible as a research tool and wondered if the computer could answer to the daunting questions provided by the president. Jessica now felt frightened by a computer that had previously fascinated her. During her youth in Fresno, California, Jessica and her family were members of a Catholic church. Since becoming an adult, Jessica continued to embrace Catholicism and occasionally went to Mass at a nearby church.

As a biochemist, Jessica considered the Universe to be God's big canvas, on which he painted the picture of eternity. Jessica wondered if Eagle Nebula would cause her to question her faith or reinforce it.

At 9 a.m. the following morning, the ACTOR team met in the lab's conference room. Everyone, except Bruce and Jessica, were tense with anticipation. Bruce began the discussion.

"As you are well aware, Jessica and I were recently at the White House at President Ramsey's request. We all know that ACTOR's achievements are numerous and recognized both nationally and internationally. We also know that it was President Ramsey who spearheaded the conception and development of this computer and whose funding is assured until the end of his term in office. Until now, ACTOR's research has focused primarily on astronomy and atomic energy. Well, that's about to change, at least temporarily. The president has requested that ACTOR be uploaded with the appropriate data, to answer three questions: What is life and does it exist elsewhere in the Universe? What is the fate of the human race, and finally, does God exist? These questions are unprecedented, controversial and perhaps unanswerable, but the president wants this project, which is top secret, to take priority over everything else. This project will be referred to as Eagle Nebula.

"I'm going to give you thirty minutes to think about this project alone, because it may make some of you uncomfortable. If you decide you don't want to participate in this project, you will be placed on leave until this project is completed. Whatever the case, however, each of you will sign a document and take an oath that you will not discuss the nature of this project with anyone outside of this room. When you return in thirty minutes, a member of the President's staff will have you sign the forms, and shortly thereafter, the president will have you take the oath, via a virtual meeting. So, I'll see you in a half hour."

Upon their return, each member of the lab signed the forms and afterwards took the oath that was administered, via video, by the president. Immediately afterwards, Bruce called each member by name to see if they were onboard with the project or taking a leave of absence. Everyone indicated they were onboard with the project.

"Let's take an hour break and when we return, we will discuss what is needed to bring this project into fruition," Bruce said.

After returning:

"Now that we are all committed to this project, does anyone have any questions or something they would like to discuss?" Bruce asked.

"I have something to say," said Evelyn.

"Go ahead, Evelyn."

"This project will surely test the limits of ACTOR's abilities, and before it can provide answers to the questions, relative to this project, it must be fed with everything we know about science, human history and theology. This may take months to complete."

"I agree. Anyone else?"

"I have an idea. Since ACTOR began functioning, it has been fed an enormous amount of data from which it has provided answers. Such being the case, perhaps we can shorten this project by seeing if ACTOR can answer at least one of the questions," said Faz.

"And what question would that be?" Jessica asked.

"Let's ask ACTOR if God exists and see if it can provide an answer," Faz said.

"How do the rest of you feel about that?" Bruce asked.

"I'm okay with it, because I'm sure ACTOR will indicate that God does not exist," said Boris.

"Boris, because you are an atheist doesn't mean this computer is one. Let's see what the computer has to say," said Howard.

"Do you want to bet on it?" Boris asked.

"Look guys, no one is betting on anything. Let's keep in mind that this is a high-level project. I'll tell you what, give me a show of hands from those who think we should submit to ACTOR the question about right now," Bruce said.

Those who raised their hands were Bruce, Faz, Evelyn and Boris. Jessica, Joe and Howard abstained.

"It's a narrow victory, but the majority wins so we will ask the computer right now. Evelyn, submit the question to ACTOR."

About ten seconds after Evelyn submitted the question, ACTOR provided an answer.

"After searching my memory banks, I have a question for you. What is God?"

Shortly thereafter, the group returned to the conference room.

"It's obvious that ACTOR cannot answer the question about God, because it has never been fed information about religion or theology. In order for it to provide an answer, this must be done," Bruce said.

"I disagree," Boris said.

"Why, Boris?"

"Correct me if I'm wrong, but I think the president wants the computer to evaluate all known scientific data to determine if God or an entity that created the Universe exists. If we upload religion and theology into the computer, its answers will probably coincide with that of humanity's," Boris replied.

"For once I agree with you, Boris," Joe said.

"Anyone else? Give me a show of hands for those who support Boris's suggestion."

Those who raised their hands were Bruce, Boris, Faz, Evelyn and Joe.

"The majority wins, so ACTOR will be free to make its own decision about the existence of God based only on scientific data. In order for the computer to answer the questions about life and the fate of humanity, it must be fed everything we know. Correct me if I miss something, but the data uploaded into the computer should include all sciences, such as physics, chemistry, biology, human anatomy, botany, cosmology, geology, meteorology, astronomy, botany and anything I fail to mention. For an answer about human fate, the computer must be fed human history, which includes religion, psychology and sociology. In other words, ACTOR must know everything we know in order to make a decision," Bruce said.

"I have a serious concern," Jessica said.

"What's that, Jessica?"

"We know that ACTOR must be fed a vast quantity of data in order to provide answers, but I have an important concern. By doing this, ACTOR will become the most omniscient non-human entity on the planet. What if the computer decides to use all this information in an unforeseen and nefarious manner?"

"That's a good point, but do you think that's possible?" Faz asked.

"I think we are in unchartered waters with this project, so anything's possible," said Howard.

"I'll tell you what, let's take two days off to think about this project and what is needed to complete it in a timely manner. But also, as a way to ensure our safety. The president wants this project completed before the end of his term, so we only have six months to work with. If there are no further questions, I will see you in three days," said Bruce.

Three days later, the group reconvened in the conference room.

"Evelyn just informed me that it will take at least four months to upload all the requisite data into ACTOR. After that, it's up to the computer to provide us the answers. Evelyn, since you're the computer whiz, give us your thoughts on the best way forward," said Bruce.

"To avoid overloading the computer, I think we should first gather all the information the computer will need, which can be loaded on the mega-drives. Afterwards, the computer will be fed in three stages, so it can digest the information in its data banks and subsequently provide us the answer. Since the first question proposed by the president is about life beyond Earth, we should collect all the data in the appropriate scientific disciplines and feed that to the computer. After we receive the answer on life, we will upload all the appropriate data on human history, which will include human psychology, sociology, religion and the humanities. After ACTOR provides the answer to the question of the fate of the human race, we will submit the final question. For the final question, ACTOR will digest all the information it's been fed, both scientific and non-scientific, to decide if God or a supreme entity exists. The final question should be: Based on information in your database, can you decide whether or not the Universe was created by a super intelligent entity or is the Universe just a random collection of matter that somehow organized itself into its present state?"

"That sounds like a great plan. Any objections or any other suggestions?" Bruce asked. Everyone expressed their approval.

"Okay. Then we will implement the plan outlined by Evelyn. I'm going to have Jessica assign each member of our team one of the disciplines, on which they will collect all the data associated with that subject and provide it to Evelyn. So, let's get started."

Over the next four months, the team gathered data for uploading into ACTOR's database. One day while the group was lunching in their breakroom, Howard made an announcement: "I, along with the rest of you, signed and took an oath, relative to this project, but I believe some things, such as religion and God, should be off-limits. I have no problem asking the computer to provide an answer regarding life or what it believes will be the fate of the human race, but not about God. There are many people, such as myself, who have strong beliefs about God and Christianity in general. My concern is that this computer, which is like a rock star to many, will shatter their beliefs, which won't be good for our society. What if ACTOR suggests there is no God or if so, that God is indifferent about the fate of humanity. Such an outcome could cause widespread civil disobedience, suicides and killings and perhaps a nuclear war. If the public becomes aware of this project, and they most likely will, the life of everyone associated with this mission will be in danger. I consider myself an Evangelical Christian and my faith will not be altered in any way by this computer's answers. Let's not forget that this computer was created by humans and is therefore fallible. I'm just afraid of the societal repercussions that may result from its answers. "

"I think we all have concerns, Howard, and let's keep in mind that whatever this computer decides, its decisions are based on the data we have provided and our data is by no means universal. For instance, we still don't know if life exists beyond earth or if there is intelligent life elsewhere in the Universe. Sure, ACTOR pointed out a site on the moon that appears to bear an unnatural form, but we can't verify with any certainty that it was made by aliens," Joe said.

"I'm glad to hear your opinion, Howard, and over the next weeks or months, I think all of us should share our thoughts about this project, but we are obligated to complete it," Bruce said.

"One thing I want to point out is that in uploading data about human history, it is impossible to delete information about the role that religion has played in shaping our history," Howard said.

"Yes. Jessica and I have talked about that. Unless you all disagree, I think we should just upload as much information about human history, including religion, into the computer and let it form its own decision. Bear in mind that ACTOR was designed to compartmentalize its assignments, so most likely it will not allow data about human history to affect its answer about the existence of God," Bruce said.

Although he signed on and took the oath, Howard was greatly troubled by the Eagle Nebula project because he felt it posed a threat to his beliefs as well as the beliefs of millions of others. Moreover, by being a self-described conservative, he never liked the liberal leaning president. Howard, his wife Lucinda and their three children, who resided in Naperville, Illinois, were deeply religious and active in a nearby church where Howard taught Sunday school and Lucinda sang in the choir. There were no secrets between Howard and Lucinda and he regularly briefed her about his non-classified projects at the lab. Howard believed his first loyalty was to God and Jesus Christ and his second was to his wife and family. In spite of taking an oath, Howard told Lucinda about Eagle Nebula.

"Lucinda, now that you know about our current project," which he declined to name, "you must promise not to discuss it with anyone."

"I promise that I won't discuss it unless you tell me otherwise. In spite of the project, I believe that our faith will prevail. What are the odds that the computer will support the beliefs of most Christians?"

"I have no idea, Lucinda, but for some reason, I think it's unlikely."

"Why do you think that?"

"ACTOR only relies on empirical and tangible facts and not beliefs or faith. "

"Since you don't support this project, why don't you just quit?"

"For one, I took an oath, and two, I need to be there until its conclusion."

"Howard, if you feel this project is a threat to Christianity, you must find a way to stop it. You must do whatever it takes and I, along with millions of others, will support you."

"Thanks, Lucinda. I will think of something."

The next day at work, Boris, who considered Howard to be a religious zealot, goaded him into an argument about God. This led to a physical altercation wherein Howard threw the first punch. Howard hoped that an altercation would create a distraction that would slow the pace of the project. If this did not work, Howard would try something else. Howard, age 40, was a few years younger, an inch or two shorter, at five feet nine, with a smaller physique than Boris. Howard's punch landed squarely on Boris's jaw. Boris was shocked, but before he could retaliate, Bruce and Joe stepped in and separated the two.

"Look guys, we can't let our disagreements affect this project nor our ability to work together. We've worked on many projects and nothing like this has ever happened before. All of us are needed to complete this project in a timely manner, but, Howard, since you started the fight, you must take the rest of the week off," Bruce said.

Without saying anything further, Howard departed the lab. Over the next few days, Howard decided he needed to do something more drastic. He decided not to tell Lucinda about the altercation or his plan to destroy the computer.

Three days later and about two hours before he would normally leave for work, Howard arose before sunrise and dressed as if he was going to work.

"Howard, why are you leaving so early?" Lucinda asked.

"We're starting a little bit earlier today, honey. Go back to sleep."

Howard went to his garage, and before entering his car, he placed two large gasoline cans that were used for the lawn mower into his trunk. Shortly after departing his house, Howard stopped at a nearby gas station and filled each can to capacity. Howard's plan was to enter the lab before everyone else, turn off the smoke alarms and set fire to ACTOR. Howard knew he would be prosecuted for arson, but he felt he needed to sacrifice himself for a greater good.

Approximately four miles from the lab, Howard's electric powered SUV approached some train tracks. Howard slowed, and as his vehicle reached the tracks, his vehicle stalled. The horn from a freight train was heard in the distance. Shortly thereafter, the warning signal came on and the crossbars lowered. Howard tried to get the vehicle started, but it failed to respond nor was he able to unlock the doors. The train crashed into Howard's SUV, turning it into a fireball and killing Howard in the process.

Within hours of the crash, the ACTOR Lab and Howard's family were notified of the accident. Bruce immediately called Lucinda to express the condolences from Howard's colleagues and to offer any assistance. Afterwards, Bruce gathered everyone into the conference room.

"Today we have lost a valuable member of our team. Such being the case, all of us will have to step it up in view of Howard's death. I expressed our condolences to Lucinda and offered her any assistance she might need."

"How is she taking it?" asked Jessica.

"I'm not so sure since our conversation was brief. But I would imagine not well. She, Howard and their kids were a close-knit family," Bruce replied.

"I hope their faith will get them through this tragedy," said Joe.

"I heard that the accident occurred just before sunrise or about 6 a.m. and on a road leading to the lab. I wonder if Howard was coming here, even though he was off until next week. Usually, Howard did not arrive here until 8:30 a.m.," said Faz.

"I would like to know his reasons as well. During my conversation with Lucinda, she said Howard was on his way to the lab. Another strange thing is that she seemed irritated that I called," Bruce said.

"Maybe he was planning to sabotage this project," said Boris.

"Hopefully that is not the case and at this point we can only speculate. For now, I think we should focus on Howard's contributions to this lab, his expertise in the field of chemistry and his work ethic. Let's work until noon and afterwards each of you may mourn his death privately," said Bruce.

Several days after Howard's death, Bruce and Jessica separately reached out to Lucinda to offer assistance and find out about her plans for a memorial service. Each of their calls went into her voicemail and their calls were not returned. A week later, the lab members read about Howard's memorial service in the local newspaper.

During a conference meeting at the lab, Bruce addressed his staff: "I think it's odd that Howard's wife did not inform us about Howard's memorial service. Howard was a member of this lab since its inception and was an integral part of our team," Bruce said.

"Maybe she felt that Howard should have been invited to the White House. I was disappointed that I wasn't invited," Evelyn said.

"I can understand your disappointment, but that was the president's call. Keep in mind, however, that we have all enjoyed the acclaim and prestige of being associated with this lab," said Jessica.

During their next informal break, Bruce gave his opinion about Eagle Nebula: "For what it's worth, I was raised as a Presbyterian, which is similar to other Protestant religions. Until I entered college,

I blindly accepted everything I was taught in church and fully embraced Christianity. Prior to entering college, my parents had encouraged me to become a pastor since I frequently read the Bible and was active in our church. Unbeknownst to them, however, was that I had a crush on a girl in our Bible study class.

"During my college years, I only went to church when I returned home and because I was urged to do so by my parents. In retrospect, the sermons I heard did vary somewhat, but overall, they were repetitious. For instance, I can't count the number of times I was told that Christ died for our sins and whoever accepts Christ as their Lord and Savior will not perish but have an everlasting life. I think most people who worship Christ embrace a concept or a vision of a man that was formulated over two thousand years ago. We have no idea what Jesus Christ actually looked like, so many people have chosen a European image of a Middle-Eastern man. While I believe in God, I find it difficult understanding the God portrayed in the Bible. For instance, why would a God described as loving allow his son to be tortured and killed, in addition to allowing wars, slavery and the Holocaust? I question how Adam and Eve's sons, Cain and Abel, found wives who were not their sisters and why God would only appear before Moses and not Pharaoh as well.

"With respect to the question about life, I believe that life exists beyond Earth and it's only a matter of time before we discover it. Thus far, Mars has been a disappointment, but the moons Europa and Enceladus seem promising, as well as Titan. As far as the fate of the human race, I think we will slowly but continually evolve on this planet for at least another million years. So, my colleagues, that is my opinion of the questions posed by Eagle Nebula."

"Why don't you tell us your beliefs, Jessica?"

"As some of you may already know, I was raised a Catholic and attended Catholic primary and secondary schools. Although, I infrequently attend church today, my beliefs have remained constant. Consequently, I believe that God created everything in the Universe and is constantly monitoring the affairs of humans. But I have some conflicts with my beliefs as a result of all the turmoil, both past and present, on Earth. I'm beginning to lean more toward an existentialistic view of God. As far as life, I think there may be life elsewhere in the Universe, but until we confirm it, I will remain a skeptic. And as far as the fate of humanity, that is beyond my concern. Right now, I have other problems to deal with."

"What are your thoughts, Joseph?" Jessica asked.

"My upbringing was comprised of parts Christianity, Islam and Animism or voodoo as some prefer to call it. Growing up in rural Tanzania, my family was more focused on survival than religion. I believe in a God, or monotheism, and I believe that while God oversees the events occurring in our world, his primary realm exists in a region that is loosely tethered to the physical Universe. When I was twelve years old, I witnessed the opening of a portal to God's world during a spiritual ritual at my home. During this occasion, my mother, who was mentally strong but physically frail and sickly, briefly succumbed to the spirit of a deceased ancestor. While being possessed by this spirit, which lasted about thirty minutes, she had to be restrained by my burly father and uncle. My mother's normally mild voice changed to a deep masculine voice, which disclosed some unknown secrets about our family and were not known to my mother beforehand.

"As far as the question of life is concerned, I believe it exists throughout the Universe and we will eventually find it when our technology enables us to travel to the far reaches of this galaxy. There are a few places in our solar system that may harbor life, but we don't have the equipment yet to verify this. As far as the fate of the human race is concerned, that is and will always be something that is unknown, as far as I'm concerned. I hope we are mindful that however ACTOR answers the three questions, these answers will only be the computer's projections based on the data it has. Even though it will process a vast amount of scientific and historical data, this data, especially the scientific data, is limited on a universal scale. For instance, every year we are learning something new in astronomy and medicine as well as the other sciences."

Shortly after Joe spoke, Evelyn informed her colleagues that the scientific data uploaded into ACTOR was nearly eighty percent complete. The only subjects remaining were botany, meteorology and the geology records of the solar systems terrestrial planets and moons. Since Howard's death, Faz and Jessica collected appropriate scientific data for uploading and Joe and Boris handled human history.

"How much time do you need to finish uploading the scientific data?" Bruce asked.

"About two weeks," responded Evelyn.

Later that week, a local newspaper reported that it had received information from an anonymous source that ACTOR was being used for a non-scientific endeavor. The national press further investigated this story and subsequently revealed that ACTOR was being used to determine if God existed. This story spread like wildfire and during his next news conference, President Ramsey was asked if the story was true.

"I'm not ready to make a comment at this time, but I will look into this matter and as soon as I know, I will inform the American people." Ramsey took no further questions and left the White House's media room.

In the following weeks, demonstrations sprouted up around the country and eventually, overseas, as protesters first demanded to know if the story was true and by not denied by the President, the demonstrations became more widespread and violent. This was exacerbated when

Ramsey beefed up security at the lab by placing the National Guard around the perimeter. Afterwards, Ramsey met with his national security team to discuss this problem.

"Does anyone know who leaked information about Eagle Nebula to the press?" Ramsey asked.

"We've interviewed and polygraphed all personnel assigned to the lab and everyone passed. We have reason to believe it was leaked by the widow of one of the scientists who worked at the lab or someone he was close to," the FBI director said.

"Has the wife been interviewed?"

"She refused to be interviewed and she was not under oath, Mr. President."

"I understand. Well, we need to do some damage control now. During my briefing with the press today, I will say that the ACTOR Laboratory is engaged in a top-secret operation that I won't discuss. End of story."

President Ramsey's announcement, however, failed to quell the demonstrations and riots occurring at home and abroad. Meanwhile, back at the lab:

"Boris, what are your thoughts about life, human fate and the existence of God?" Bruce asked.

"I have no objections to this mission and I am anxious to hear the computer's answers to these questions. As far as the question about life is concerned, I think the computer will suggest there is life elsewhere in the Universe, but we just have to find it. I don't think ACTOR will be able to answer the question about the fate of humanity and I have no opinion on that. Personally, I'm an atheist and I believe that the concept of God is a human invention. I grew up in Russia and my parents were atheists. The only time I've ever been inside a church was for a friend's wedding. Overall, I think religion is a waste of time and money, although it may benefit people who suffer from psychological maladies, such as depression or low self-esteem. Imagine how much more advanced we would be if the money we spend on religions were spent on medical and scientific research.

"If you look back in human history, the ancients believed that many Gods existed. The Greeks and Egyptians worshiped a number of Gods and even considered their Pharaoh to be a God. Later, other cultures created their version of God, with Western societies embracing Christianity. The Christian Bible says God created man in his image, but in reality, Christians created a God, along with a sub-God in Jesus Christ."

"How about you, Faz, what's your opinion?" Boris asked.

"I agree with Boris that life does exist beyond Earth and it's just a matter of time before we find it. As far as the fate of the human race is concerned, I believe that humans will survive on this planet for at least a million more years, if not longer. But in the process, we will slowly evolve into creatures with far superior intellectual ability.

"I was raised in India and my parents were Hindus. In spite of my education, my wife and I continue to worship that religion. As a Hindu, I accept Brahman as our universal God, in addition to three deities. I also believe in reincarnation, which is at the heart of my religion. I seriously doubt if ACTOR will cause me to change or drop my religious beliefs, but I am interested in hearing what the computer concludes. I think everyone except Evelyn has given their opinion about this project. What's her opinion?"

"I'll see if she can join us," Jessica said. A few moments later, Evelyn entered the break room and provided her opinion about Eagle Nebula.

"Look, guys, I'm crazy busy right now uploading a huge amount of data into the computer so we can complete this project and return to what we do best. But since you want to hear my thoughts, I will say that it's quite likely that life exists elsewhere in this vast Universe. I think we will eventually find it if it hasn't already found us. Right now, I have no opinion on the fate of the human race, but if I were to give an estimate, I would say that humans will thrive on this planet for no more than another one hundred thousand years.

"Basically, I'm an agnostic who learned about God in a Methodist church. Over time, I became less religious, and although I believe there is a God, I'm not sure about his nature or character. If we look at the history of life on Earth, life has evolved and so perhaps has God. After all, he had dinosaurs before he created us humans. I don't know what the outcome of this project will be, but I hope that ACTOR can help humanity evolve our concept of God. The demonstrations and rioting that are occurring right now are caused by people who fear science as well as learning something new. God created this awesome Universe and the more we know about the Universe, the more we will know about the God who created it. The Bible only tells you a limited version of a one-dimensional God. Maybe ACTOR can increase our insight."

CHAPTER FIVE

During their time away from the lab, the scientists addressed matters in their personal lives. Some of their problems resulted from the controversy associated with Eagle Nebula. For instance, Jessica, who had not heard from her daughter since she went to China, decided to use her contacts within the White House to have the State Department look into this matter. At some point, Jessica received an early morning call from the U.S. Embassy in Beijing, China.

"Hi, is this Jessica Minton?"

"Yes. Who's calling?

"Hi, I'm Warren Dixon, with the U.S. Embassy in China. I have some news about your daughter, Shensi."

"Great. I haven't heard from her in nearly a month. Is she okay?"

"She's alive, but she's been arrested for spying and has been incarcerated for the past four weeks. That's why you haven't heard from her."

"How could she be arrested for spying? She was just touring China and trying to locate her biological parents. Is there any way you can get her released?"

"That's what we're working on. As you're probably aware, there are tensions between the United States and China, which makes it somewhat risky to visit here. Apparently, Shensi went to a remote village and began questioning people about her family. Someone notified the authorities who subsequently arrested Shensi. During their interrogation of her, she identified you as her adoptive parent and they learned from their investigation that you are a scientist on the most advanced computer in the world. They may eventually release her but not until they get something in return. As we speak, President Ramsey and the State Department are negotiating with the Chinese to have her released and returned home."

"How long do you think that will take?"

"I can't say, but I assure you we are doing everything we can."

"Is there any way I can talk to Shensi?"

"I will try to arrange that, but if I do, please limit your conversation with her to only her wellbeing. Do not discuss your work, the negotiations or anything else. Do you understand?"

"Yes."

"If I'm successful, I will give you a heads up on when to expect her call."

"Thanks, Mr. Dixon."

The following day, Jessica received a call from Dixon, who told her to expect a call from Shensi within the hour.

"Hi, Mom, this is Shensi."

"Hi, Shensi. I've been so worried about you and I'm so sorry you've been arrested. How are you doing?"

"I'm doing okay, but this is not a pleasant ordeal. I pray they will let me out of here."

"How's the food?"

"It's barely tolerable. Look, Mom, they're saying I have to end my call, so pray for me and I love you. Goodbye, Mom."

After the extremely brief call, Jessica cried for a moment and then called Bruce to inform him about Shensi. Knowing how distressed she was, Bruce told her to take a few days off.

Four weeks later, Shensi was released from jail and she immediately returned to the United States. Shensi never located her natural parents.

Shortly after graduating from college, Faz married Dapa Akbar, a nursing student, whom he had met a year earlier after being introduced by a friend. The couple had two children, who were now adults. Their son was an oral surgeon and resided in Atlanta, Georgia, and their daughter worked for a software company in California's Silicon Valley. Faz, now fifty-five, and Dapa, fifty-three, lived not far from the lab, in Bolingbrook, Illinois.

Upon returning home one evening, Faz noticed that someone had moved into the house next door, which had been for sale. Faz was an avid gardener, and one Saturday morning, while tending to his garden, he had his first encounter with the new neighbor. The neighbor was an attractive young woman in her late twenties and of Indian descent. Upon seeing Faz, the woman walked over to a shrub bordering their property and introduced herself. Faz was immediately taken by her long black hair, bronze skin, hazel eyes and finely chiseled body, clad in a tight- fitting dress.

"Hi, I'm Nischa, your new neighbor."

"Hi, Nischa. I'm Fazlur, but please call me Faz. Your place has been emptying for several months so I'm glad it's found a buyer. Do you live alone?"

"Yes, I do. And you?"

"I live with my wife who's a registered nurse at the hospital. What type of work do you do?"

"I'm employed at a modeling firm and I work part-time as an exotic dancer."

"That's interesting. I've never met an exotic dancer before."

"It's just a temporary job for now. If you are interested in seeing me perform, I work evenings at Flexibles."

"I would love to, but my wife would not approve of it."

"I understand. What do you do for a living?

"I work at the Fermi Lab."

"That sounds interesting. What do you do there?"

"I'm one of the scientists."

"I'm impressed. You must be a brilliant man. "

"Thanks, but overall, I'm quite boring."

"Speaking of boring, can I trouble you to see why I have no electric power in my kitchen?"

"It may be your circuit breaker. Let's go check and see."

Faz followed Nischa into her home, which was sparsely decorated and with little furniture other than a couch, in the living room. After checking the switches in her kitchen, he asked her to lead him to the basement. After locating the circuit breaker box, he flipped the switch for her kitchen. Upon returning to the kitchen, Nischa's electric power was restored.

"Thanks for helping me, Faz."

"Any time, Nischa. If you need help with anything else, don't hesitate to ask."

Faz was so mesmerized by Nischa that he began checking to see if she were home when Dapa was away at work. Usually, Nischa was not home, but one evening she was.

"Hi, Nischa, I was just checking to see if there were any more problems with your house or if you needed my help with anything."

"No, not that I can think of, but since you are here, I would like your opinion on something."

"Sure. No problem."

Afterwards, Nischa led Faz to her sparsely furnished bedroom, which contained just a bed and a small dresser.

"What, do you have a problem with this room?" Faz asked somewhat nervously.

"Sit on the bed and make yourself comfortable. I want you to critique me on a new erotic dance I'm performing."

Before Faz could answer, Nischa dimmed the bedroom light, played some soft music and started her dance routine. By the time Nischa removed the last of her clothing, Faz was horny and raring to go, because he and Dapa had sex far less than he preferred.

"You look like you could use a glass of water."

"Yes."

Nischa departed the room in her birthday suit and shortly returned with a paper cup filled with water.

"I'm sorry I don't have bottled water. I'm slowly buying the things I need to transform this place into a proper home."

After Faz finished drinking the water, Nischa, observing that he had an erection, sat beside him and began undressing him. Nischa then reached into her purse and extracted a condom for Faz. After a moment of kissing and caressing, they had sexual intercourse and then fell asleep.

Hours later, Nischa awoke, got dressed, placed her toiletries and belongings into a suitcase and quietly left.

When Dapa returned home the next morning, she noticed that Faz's car was still in the garage and the house was eerily quiet. Since Faz often got up early to work in the garden, Dapa went to their back yard, where she noticed that the gate was open and Faz's garden tools were on the ground. Wondering why this was so, she went to the adjacent house to see if he was there. Dapa proceeded to knock on the door, but there was no response. After retrieving her cellphone, Dapa called Faz's number and heard it ringing inside the home, but still, no response. After a series of knocks and yelling Faz's name, Dapa decided to call the police.

When the police arrived, an officer questioned Dapa about Faz and why she thought he was in this particular house.

"Ms. Pandit, why would your husband come to this home? Was he visiting someone here?

"Not that I'm aware of. This house has been vacant for months."

"I was just informed by my department who checked with the realty agency that this home is for sale and uninhabited. If someone was staying here, they were squatters. When you dialed your husband's cellphone, we can hear it ringing inside, so someone must have let him in. A realty agent will be here shortly."

As soon as the realty agent arrived, the two police officers entered the house, but told the agent and Dapa to wait outside. After about ten or so minutes, one of the officers came out to inform Dapa that Faz was in the house, but he was deceased. Dapa became hysterical and the officer tried to console her. After calming her down, the officer asked her some questions.

"Miss, do you have any idea why your husband was in this house or who he was seeing here?"

"I have no idea why he was here. Do you think someone else was here?"

"Right now, we don't know, but we will conduct an investigation to determine if your husband was visiting and if he was a victim of foul play."

"Why do you say that? Do you think he was killed?"

"This may upset you, but there's something else you should know. Your husband, whom we will need you to identify, was lying on a bed nude and wearing a condom. Apparently, he was having sexual relations with someone here. A neighbor said she saw a young woman entering this house a few days ago, so we will try to find out her identity, in addition to finding out the cause of your husband's death. Since there's no visible evidence of foul play, the coroner will have to determine the cause of his death."

Soon afterwards, more police cars and an ambulance arrived at the scene. At some point Faz's body was removed from the house and Dapa was allowed to see his face. Dapa acknowledged it was her husband. Upon returning home, Dapa called her children, relatives, friends and Bruce. Later, the coroner determined that Faz's cause of death was a heart attack. DNA from the woman who identified herself as Nischa was recovered in the house and on Faz's body, she was never located.

The following day, Bruce hastily arranged for a meeting in the lab's conference room.

"I hate to bring you more bad news, but last night Faz's wife called to let me know that he had died from a heart attack. Faz was a good person, an esteemed scientist and his presence here will be greatly missed."

"You've got to be kidding. He was only fifty-five and appeared to be in good shape. Did his wife give any details on how he died?" Boris asked.

"All she said was that he died at home in his sleep."

"Boy, this is really a shocker. First Howard and now Faz. Fortunately for the sake of this project, just about everything has been uploaded into ACTOR," Jessica said.

President Ramsey was conferring with the Secretary of State, along with other members of his staff, on Air Force One, during a return flight to Washington D.C. Over the past five days, Ramsey had met with several Asian leaders to discuss environmental and economic matters. While over the Pacific Ocean, at about forty thousand feet, an object, possibly space debris or a meteorite, struck the starboard wing of the airplane. The impact destabilized the plane, causing it to abruptly descend about twenty thousand feet. All the passengers who were not strapped in were tossed about, with some suffering non-life-threatening injuries. Ramsey suffered a broken arm, and the Secretary of State, among others, suffered concussions. Although the wing suffered significant damage, the pilots were able to stabilize the plane long enough to make an emergency landing in Hawaii. Ramsey and those suffering injuries were treated at hospitals in Honolulu. Ramsey returned to Washington four days later.

Back at the lab, the scientists discussed this incident.

"That must have been a terrifying ordeal for the president. Fortunately, this was not a disaster. There's been enough heartbreak around here," Jessica said.

"I wonder what would have become of this project had he not survived?" asked Boris.

"Who knows. With all the turmoil going on in the country, I think the vice president would have killed this project," Joe said.

"I'm inclined to agree," said Boris.

Shortly thereafter, Evelyn entered the breakroom to make an announcement. "ACTOR is fully loaded, and if my calculations are correct, it should have an answer for the question about life within a week or so," Evelyn said.

CHAPTER SIX

Ten days later, ACTOR revealed its answer to the question about life:

"After evaluating all the information supplied to my database, that was derived from the physical sciences, such as chemistry, physics, biology, botany, astronomy, microbiology, geology, meteorology, etc., I have concluded that there are numerous forms of life. The most basic form of life is atomic life, which underscores every particle in the Universe. Atomic life is at the root of every particle of matter and it ranges in size to the simplest element, hydrogen, to the largest stars. Other forms of life are nuclear life, which powers the stars, geological life, which drives the outer layers of terrestrial planets, such as Earth. There's meteorological or atmospheric life, which is common to all planets bearing an atmosphere. There's hydraulic life, which is common to all liquids, whether it's a glass of water, to the liquid interiors of most planets such as Earth, Jupiter, Neptune, etc. There is also chemical life, which may be found on planets such as Jupiter, Saturn, Uranus, Neptune and Saturn's moon Titan. And of course, there's the form of life that humans recognize as the only form of life and that is bio-chemical life. Other forms of life are thermal and radioactive and electromagnetic. In essence, everything in the Universe is some form of life, which makes the Universe a living organism.

"In addition to the above, I've also calculated that there's a less detectable form of life that's supernatural in nature. Examples of supernatural life are the regions within the event horizon of a black hole, dark energy, gravity and space-time. Another omnipresent but even less detectable form of life is spiritual life. For example, the dreams that humans have are a brief portal to the spiritual world."

After hearing and recording ACTOR's response to the question of life, the scientists met in the conference room to voice their opinions relative to this answer. Bruce began first.

"Well now we have the computer's answer regarding life. I've never viewed life as broadly as ACTOR and most if not, all scientists consider life as it's conceived on Earth and that is biochemical in nature. What about you, Jessica?"

"I'm shocked by ACTOR's answer and would like to give it more thought. But I have to agree that we humans do view life quite narrowly. When you really think about it, the tiniest particle of matter bears energy, so in a sense it is alive."

"Like you, Jessica, I need more time to process this. I think ACTOR's answers are quite controversial and will certainly cause some heated debates within the scientific community as well as with religious groups. But what really surprises me is ACTOR indicating the existence of metaphysical and supernatural life. Astronomers have observed events in the Universe that defy physics, such as black holes, the big bang and dark energy but we scientists prefer to call it something more palatable," Joe said. "What about you, Boris?"

"I'm somewhat overwhelmed by ACTOR's answer to the question of life but given enough time and thought, I believe I can accept it. And you, Evelyn?"

"Like the rest of you, I'm astonished by this answer. I'll leave it at that for now. Now that the answer to the first question is out of the way, I will direct the computer to process the enormous amount of data on human history, anatomy, sociology and psychology, religion so it can provide its answer on the fate of the human race."

"How long do you think that will take, Evelyn?" Bruce asked.

"Two to three weeks, I guess. Just so you know, this project is putting a strain on the computer because it was not designed to process so much data in such a short period of time. To compensate, I'm going to lower the temperature in the lab by about five degrees because ACTOR is generating more heat than usual."

"Do whatever you think is necessary, Evelyn. By the way, Faz's wife called me this morning to say thank you for the letters of condolences and flowers you sent. She also said the FBI is conducting a criminal investigation on Faz's death. Apparently, a toxicology exam revealed that a foreign chemical in his blood caused his heart attack. Moreover, Dapa disclosed that just before he died, Faz had sex with some mystery woman. They recovered the woman's DNA but haven't determined her identity," Bruce said.

"Sex is not a bad way to end one's life, but not if it's artificially induced. I feel sorry for Faz and his family. In spite of his fatal indiscretion, Faz was a good man who did not deserve to die like this. Why would someone want to kill him?" Joe asked.

"No one knows for sure, but because of the controversial nature of this project, the FBI suspects that his death was intentional. I spoke to Hogan about this and he urges us to be very careful when we are away from the lab. He recommended we be wary of strangers, enhance our home's security and while driving, check to see if you're being followed. Fortunately, there aren't many protesters around here anymore, but be careful and always use the rear entrance to this facility," Bruce said.

Just as Bruce ended his conversation, Lena buzzed the conference room.

"Folks, may I come in for a minute? I have an announcement to make." Shortly thereafter, Lena entered the conference room.

"Most of you don't know this, but in the past, I've had two miscarriages. Well, I'm pregnant again and just finished my first trimester. So far, things are looking good, but my physician and my husband think I should stay at home for the balance of my pregnancy. So, beginning Monday, I'm going to work from my residence, and if everything goes well, I should return to the lab in about ten months."

"Your presence will be missed by all of us, Lena, and best of luck with your pregnancy. Let me know if you need anything from us," Bruce said.

When Joe entered his home after a day at the lab, it was eerily quiet inside and his three-year-old son Joey was not there to greet him. Joe called Jill's name and looked through the house, but no one was there. Joe then checked his cell phone to see if Jill left him a message, which she had not. Joe then called Jill's cell phone, which went into her voicemail. Joe left a message and expected a return call within minutes, but it never came.

Joe ate some leftovers, took a shower and returned to his bedroom. Nothing like this had ever occurred before and he knew of no issues with their relationship. However, recently Jill did seem troubled by something, but when asked she said it was nothing important. At some point, Joe opened the drawer to her night table and upon doing so he saw an envelope addressed to him and bearing Jill's handwriting. Joe opened the letter which conveyed the following message:

Joe, I'm sure by now, you are wondering where Joey and I are. I'm sorry I did not tell you this in person, but I felt it was better this way. While you are reading this note, Joey and I are on a one-way flight to Mongolia. There's a lot of things about me you do not know, including my nationality which is Mongolian and not Nepalese, which I led you to believe. Moreover, my real name is not Jill Chong, but Kubla Urtai. You are welcome to come and visit Joey and me, and if you do, I will explain why I left in this manner. Your son and I will reside near a village called Javarthushuu. Love, Jill.

Joe reread the note several times to ensure he was reading it correctly and to fully digest what he had read. Joe's feelings wandered from sadness to anger. He was furious that Jill had the audacity to take their son away without his permission or consent. He also wondered why Jill would lie about her nationality and identity and if she really loved him or had used him for some unknown purpose. Before going to bed, Joe checked Jill and Joey's closets to convince himself that they were gone. Joe observed that the bulk of their belongings were missing. Joe thought about calling someone, but to his knowledge, Jill had no close friends or family.

After lying down, Joe, who was unable to sleep, thought about how he met Jill. The meeting occurred four years ago and shortly after Joe had moved from London, England to Naperville, Illinois, following his appointment to the ACTOR lab. One morning when he stopped to enjoy a cup of coffee and a pastry at a small coffee shop in town, Jill, whom he had never seen before, came in and appeared to be looking for someone. After ordering a cup of coffee, Jill turned to survey the shop, which was crowded at the time. At some point, Jill came over to Joe's table, which had an empty chair, and asked if he would mind her sitting there. Joe was delighted because Jill was a very attractive, twenty-something, well-dressed female with Oriental features. Jill introduced herself, was quite gregarious, and Joe immediately liked her. Jill said she was new to the area and had moved here from San Francisco. During their subsequent conversation, Jill asked Joe what he did for a living and Jill said she was temporarily working at a boutique shop in town. After dating a few times, they married four months after they first met. Since they had no friends or family in the area, they married at the city hall.

Within months of their marriage, Jill became pregnant and ceased working, which had Joe's approval. Joe recalled that Jill was always interested in his work. Jill, however, seemed quite irritated when Joe refused to discuss Eagle Nebula. In fact, Jill refused to have sex with Joe until he gave her details about his latest project, which he refused to do. Joe wondered if this was the reason behind her departure.

When Joe returned to the lab the next morning, he informed his colleagues in the breakroom about the sudden and mysterious departure of his wife and son. Because of this, Joe said he needed to take some time off to go and try to retrieve his family. Bruce said this would not be a problem since ACTOR was fully uploaded and was only processing data for the remaining questions.

"Joe, I'm sorry about your wife absconding with your son. Have you made plans for your trip to Mongolia?" Boris asked.

"Not yet. I will do so as soon as I return home."

"I don't know if you are aware of this, but Mongolia is a difficult place to visit. Trying to enter the country from China is arduous and quite difficult. Plus, our relations with China aren't so good and you see what happened to Jessica's daughter. "

"I understand. What do you suggest I do?"

"I think your best bet is to fly to Moscow, Russia and from there, take a flight to Irkutsk, which is a city in eastern Russia. I still have family there and I can arrange for them to get you the necessary documents to enter Mongolia. Plus, you will need a vehicle to get to Javarthushuu."

"Thanks, Boris. I really appreciate that. As soon as I get home, I will contact my travel agent and have her book my flights to Moscow and Irkutsk."

"Okay and while you are doing that, I will contact my cousin and explain your situation. After I speak to him, I will text you his information and afterwards, let him know when to expect you."

"Sounds great and thanks again."

After making travel arrangements the following day, Joe went to the bank to withdraw some funds and discovered that Jill had withdrawn seventy percent of the nearly one hundred thousand dollars he had in their joint account. While not totally surprised, it only added to his anger. The more he revisited their time together, the more he questioned whether Jill actually loved him or if he was part of some master scheme. Joe hoped to find the answers when he met Jill in person, because her phone service was now disconnected.

Following the long flight to Irkutsk, with layovers in Amsterdam and Moscow, Joe retrieved his suitcases and exited the terminal. It was mid-August and the temperature was in the seventies. His wristwatch indicated 4 p.m. in Irkutsk, a sprawling city of about six hundred and fifty thousand people, none of whom looked like Joe, with his dark brown skin. After standing about twenty minutes, Joe was approached by a heavy-set white female, appearing to be in her forties, with blond hair, pale blue eyes and an overall forgettable appearance. Joe imagined her as a female version of Boris.

"You must be Joe. Hi, I'm Svetlana, Boris's cousin," the woman said, with a heavy accent.

"Hi, Svetlana. Joe I am."

"Well welcome to Irkutsk. Is this your first trip to Russia?"

"Not quite. About seven years ago while on a vacation, I visited St. Petersburg. By the way, Boris said the cousin that was meeting me here was a male. What happened?"

"My brother Alex was not able to come, so he asked me to assist you."

"How did you like St. Petersburg?"

"It was quite fascinating, especially the palaces of the czars."

"Well, it's too bad this isn't a vacation trip for you. Boris told me why you are here and I will do as much as I can to help you. First, I will give you a quick tour of Irkutsk and then we will go to my home, which is about thirty miles from here. I know you must be tired from the long flight and jet lag, so my suggestion is that you take at least two days to adjust before heading into Mongolia. I have a truck you can use, and after you are rested, I will brief you on what you need to know before entering Mongolia."

"Thanks, Svetlana. I appreciate all the help I can get and let me know if there's anything I can do for you."

"Just have a safe and successful trip."

Svetlana lived alone in a small cottage in a semi-rural area southeast of Irkutsk. The first day there, Joe mostly ate and did some light exercising while Svetlana was at work. When she returned home during the afternoon of his second day in Irkutsk, she had converted the money he had given her for his use in Mongolia. After dinner, Svetlana briefed Joe on Mongolian culture and what he needed to know in order to have a successful trip.

"Overall, Mongolia is a nice place to visit and the people are friendly. They will be especially curious about you since they don't see many people of African descent. The town you are visiting is about three hundred and sixty miles from here. In America, that's not a big deal because of highway system. The roads leading to Javarthushuu are a mixed bag of paved and unpaved tarmac. The landscape is interesting, but mostly stark and sparsely populated with nomadic people. I'm allowing you to use my little truck, which is two decades old, but it is reliable and should get you there and back with no problems. A full tank should carry you about four hundred miles and I'm giving you an extra four liters in a gas can. I'm sure there's a gas station in Javarthushuu, so fill up before returning. I suggest that you leave here before sunrise, because it will be around midnight when you get there. I will give you some snacks and drinking water to take, and expect to urinate or whatever on the side of the road. I want to caution you that if for some reason you find yourself travelling after nightfall and have a problem with the truck, stay inside until sunrise. The wolves are very bad in Mongolia and cellphones are useless. Do you have any questions?"

"None that I can think of, and thanks for the advice."

Early the next morning, after having a light breakfast with Svetlana, Joe departed for Mongolia, using a map she had provided him. At times, the going was slowed due to the road's gravel surface, disabled vehicles, animals crossing the road and the mountainous terrain. When Joe finally reached Javarthushuu, it was about 11 p.m. The village was dark and only a few homes were illuminated from within.

Since it was late and there were no hotels around, in addition to the fact that he did not have Jill's address, Joe had no choice but to sleep in the truck. Just before falling to sleep, Joe hoped that Jill had not lied to him about living here, because if she had, this would be a meaningless and expensive trip.

Joe was awakened the next morning by the sound of a car horn from across the street from where he was parked. Joe looked at his watch, which showed 8:23 a.m. Joe removed some photos of Jill from his suitcase and exited the truck. Joe walked toward the center of town, which bore a mixture of gravel and dirt streets and shabby, one-story commercial/residential dwellings. It was Saturday morning and only a few people were outdoors. The air was cool and Joe was hungry. He entered a small shop that was occupied by a handful of people and ordered coffee and some kind of pastry. When he finished eating, he approached the cashier and displayed a photo of Jill, with her birth name written on the back. Joe had to make gestures because he could not speak or understand the Mongolian language. The cashier shook his head and proceeded to show the photo to the customers. One customer, an elderly man, nodded and motioned for Joe to follow him. After an exchange of gestures, Joe got into his truck and followed the man who drove about a mile or so away from town. At some point, the man stopped, pointed his hand at a nearby home and drove away.

The house was a sprawling, one-story brick structure that was a significant upgrade in appearance over the other homes in the area. Joe walked to the house and knocked on the door. After a minute or so, a short, petite woman with Mongoloid features and long gray hair, appearing to be in her sixties, opened the door. Without saying a word, she motioned for Joe to come in and have a seat. Afterwards, she yelled something that Joe did not understand, that was followed by the patter of feet from the rear of the house. Before long, Jill and Joey emerged. Joey ran towards his dad and Joe scooped him up.

"Even though it hasn't been that long, it's so nice seeing you again, Joey." After a few moments of hugging Joey, Joe put his son down and Jill reluctantly stepped forward. Joe gave her a light embrace and she whispered in his ear, "I know you have a lot on your mind, but let's talk later, okay?"

"Sure. I don't plan on leaving anytime soon."

"Good and I am so glad you are here, and knowing how persistent you are, I sort of expected it. This is my mother. Just call her Ma. Let me introduce you to my father, who's bedridden and not expected to live much longer."

Jill led Joe to her father's bedroom, where he gave a weak smile and nodded at Joe, following her introduction. Afterwards, Jill gave him a tour of the house, which she said was constructed with money she sent her parents three years ago. Joe got settled in, and early that evening, Jill's two brothers, along with their wives and children, arrived carrying food for a family dinner. After they departed, Jill and Joe went for a walk.

"Joe, I know you are angry about the way I departed, and I apologize and am very sorry for doing that, but I had no choice. I will explain by starting from the beginning. When we met for the first time in that coffee shop, that meeting may have appeared to be natural to you, but it wasn't. Days earlier, I was approached by three men and one woman who said they would pay me $100,000 if I could start a relationship with you, plus another $100,000 if that relationship progressed into a marriage. I asked why and they said that you were a person of extraordinary interest because of your employment at the Fermi Lab. They knew your schedule and that you frequented the coffee shop. They said they had sent four other women to try and ignite a relationship with you, but they all failed. Do you recall anything like that happening about four years ago?"

"Come to think of it, over a succession of weeks, a few attractive women did approach me in the shop and I briefly thought I was the luckiest guy in the world. But they came across as phony and two were not particularly attractive. The other two, while attractive, had little in the way of conversation and could not remember my name when they returned to the coffee shop. So, I take it that you were the fifth woman to work for them?"

"Apparently so. Fortunately, there was some chemistry between us and I genuinely liked you. I want you to know that even though our introduction was predicated on a scam, I truly grew to love you and I still do. The reason I agreed to participate in their project was because my father had become disabled and my mother was struggling to survive here. The money I received from them was used to build this house and provide a comfortable living for my parents. In return, I was required to give these people regular updates on your projects at the Fermi Lab. "

"So that's why you frequently questioned me about my work. I thought you were just interested in science and wanted to converse about it."

"I was always interested in everything about you, but I was also liable to them. Unfortunately, things turned sour when it was rumored in the press that your team was working on a top-secret project. When I asked you about it, you said you had taken an oath and could not discuss it. I relayed this to them and they gave me an ultimatum. Either get details of your project or they would harm me and our son. After repeatedly telling them you would not provide any information, they said I had to either repay the $200,000 or they would take Joey. That is the reason why I left the way I did. I hope you understand and can forgive me."

"Why didn't you seek help from law enforcement?"

"Because I didn't know the identities of these people and they always met me at a different location. Plus, I would probably be in trouble for accepting money in that fashion and I couldn't risk anything happening to Joey."

"I understand, but I just wish you'd discussed this with me."

"Again, I apologize, but I think this was the best way forward."

"So where do we go from here? Do you and Joey plan on returning with me to the United States?"

"I can't under the circumstances. It's still too dangerous and I'm sure those folks are looking for me. "

"Well, what are your future plans?"

"I plan on Joey and I living here for the foreseeable future. My dad won't be around long and my mother needs my help. I will home school Joey until he is ready for a private school. Life in the U.S is hectic, and for now, this is where I need to be. I hope you will join us here and if not, you can visit as often as you'd like."

"Jill, I love you and Joey, but due to my work and career, there's nothing in Mongolia for me. What would you expect me to do here?"

"I understand, but I was hoping we could stay together here for at least a few years and then return to the United States or somewhere else. When we returned, however, we would have to live somewhere other than Illinois."

"Jill, this is a lot to digest, but I will think about it."

Joe spent the next few nights in bed with Jill, even though he was troubled by her decision to live in Mongolia. He slept with her because at the time, his horniness overpowered his anger. By the fourth day, Joe decided he would leave Mongolia and take Joey with him. Knowing that Jill would not allow this and he was on her turf, he had to devise a plan without arousing her suspicions.

In what he decided would be his final night in Mongolia, Joe told Jill that he wanted to spend his last night there, alone with Joey. She agreed, and around 4 a.m., Joe dressed quietly and placed his belonging in the truck. He then returned to the house and brought out Joey, who was still asleep and clad in pajamas.

Earlier that day Joe stashed away some of Joey's belongings, along with the water and snacks they would need for the return trip to Russia. After securing Joey in the second-row seat, Joe started up the truck and away they went. Joe figured it would be at least three hours before Jill awoke and discovered they were gone.

The trip back to Russia was just as slow and tedious as it was before. There were many delays and it took about several hours to cover a hundred miles. When Joey awoke, he was fed with snacks and water and told that they were taking a short trip. By 9 p.m. it was dark and there were many potholes in the road. They were about sixty miles from the Russian border when the front driver's side wheel collapsed. Joe got out of the truck to inspect the wheel and saw that a tie rod had broken. In the distance, Joe saw the lights from a nomadic compound. Seeing that Joey was asleep, Joe turned off the engine, locked the doors and walked toward the compound.

The next morning, just after daybreak, Jill and her brothers arrived where Joe's vehicle was left on the side of the road. They looked in, awakened Joey and showed him how to unlock the door. Jill and Joey got back in her brother's truck while her brothers went to look for Joe. They returned to Jill about twenty minutes later, bearing grim expressions. One of the brothers took Jill away from the truck to tell her that Joe had been severely mauled and killed by some wolves. Later, they arranged for Joe's remains to be transported back to Javarthushuu, where he was buried in the family's cemetery.

CHAPTER SEVEN

Around two weeks after Joe's last day at the lab, Bruce received a letter at the lab, informing him of Joe's death. The letter did not provide any details of Joe's death, only stating that he "died of natural causes." Immediately after reading the letter, Bruce hastily called for a meeting.

"This morning I received a letter from Joe's wife, informing us of his death. The letter provided no details and Jill indicated that he died of natural causes. That's hard to believe because Joe appeared to be in excellent health. In fact, he recently told me he passed his last physical with flying colors."

"This is terrible news. There are only eight people assigned to this lab and Joe is the third person to die this year. I believe his death should be investigated," Evelyn said.

"Well, I'm going to inform Director Hogan about his death and maybe he can have our embassy in Mongolia look into it," Bruce said.

"Joe was a fine fellow and a true friend. Somehow, I feel responsible for his death. Maybe I should have discouraged him from going to Mongolia. He was quite angry about the situation with his wife and son and maybe this contributed to his death. My cousin who assisted Joe has some friends in Mongolia, so I'm going to see if she can find out what actually happened to him," Boris said.

"Joe will certainly be missed. Fortunately, there's nothing more to do with ACTOR, other than wait for the computer's answers," Jessica said.

A few days later, ACTOR answered the question about the fate of the human race:

"After reviewing the data I received relating to human history, psychology, sociology, among other relevant subjects, I have concluded that the human race will cease to exist on this planet in no more than one thousand years. My answer is based on a number of factors and trends. For one, the number of divisions and subdivisions among humans continues to grow. Marriages are declining and consequently, fewer children are being born. Because of the death rate from cancer and other communicative diseases, the overall human population is beginning to level off and will start to decline before the end of this century. There were once just males and females, but those genders are subdividing into various groups which will increase the disintegration of the atomic family. Further destruction will result from the extreme political, ethnic and religious divisions and the increasing number of nation states. For example, there are now twice as many nations than there were a century ago and these divisions, along with dwindling natural resources, will bring about more conflicts, wars and death.

"Environmental factors will also play a role in the demise of the human race. Such factors as global warming, air and water pollution will result in a sharp decrease in agriculture. Global warming will bring on more lethal viruses and bacteria as well as hurricanes and forest fires. Moreover, the technology humans are addicted to will contribute to your demise. Electromagnetic radiation from cell phones, electric cars, computers and other electronic devices will contribute to the fatality rate from cancer and slowly sterilize human reproductive organs.

"Humans rate themselves as intelligent, but in actuality, humans are quasi-intelligent. If humans were fully intelligent, there would be no social, ethnic, racial, political, geopolitical and economic divisions or gender biases. These inherent weaknesses will prevent humans from reaching their full potential."

Immediately after hearing ACTOR'S answer, the scientists met in the conference room.

"Wow. I'm blown away by that answer. I expected humans would thrive on this planet for at least 100,000 more years. But I am concerned about all the divisions in the world that seem to keep multiplying. Parts of the South are threatening to secede, as well as Alaska and Hawaii. And that's just in the United States," Jessica said.

"I never thought about it until this project, but let's remember that ACTOR's answer is merely conjecture based on current trends. Overall, humans are quite resilient and I believe we will continue to inhabit this planet for at least another million years. But who knows what society will look like in the near future, let alone one thousand years. For most of human history, marriage was between a man and a woman. Today, marriages between heterosexuals are declining and divorces are increasing. Consequently, fewer children are being born than in the past."

"I'm not as optimistic as you guys, but I think we will exist much longer than ACTOR believes. It will be interesting to see how the public responds to this answer. Maybe something positive will come out of this and humans will set aside some of our social and political divisions. I am however, concerned about the environment and the increasing number of pandemics. I'm also concerned about the divisions that limit world peace and progress. Divisions do not bring about unity," Bruce said.

"I think ACTOR is on to something, and as pessimistic as it sounds, this is something we need to take seriously. Look at the global conflicts over strategic, but limited elements, such as iridium, cobalt and lithium. Plus, every advancement in technology has some serious drawbacks. The nuclear fusion reactors, for example, are a godsend for supplying our ever-growing energy needs, but any error in the fusion process can have devastating consequences," Evelyn said.

When Bruce called Director Hogan to inform him about Joe's death, Hogan expressed his regret and asked if he could meet privately with Bruce, in two days. Bruce agreed and the two met later for lunch at a Thai restaurant in Naperville.

"Bruce, I know you've taken an oath relative to this project assigned to you and your team by the president. According to the news media, this project has something to do with the search for God. There are other rumors, as well as conspiracy theories and none of them bode well for ACTOR's future or your job security."

"What's your question, Director?"

"Off the record, I want to know what this project is about. As the Director of the ACTOR Lab, this is something I should be privy to."

"You know I can't discuss that, and it's unfortunate the president put us in this position. But I'm the one who would go to jail if I told you the nature of this project. For all I know, we may be under surveillance right now. What is it with you and the president anyway?"

"He's angry that I backed his opponent in the last election."

"Why would you do that?"

"While I appreciate president appointing me to be the director, I never liked him or his policies. That's the short answer."

"Well, I'm sorry and there's nothing more I can say."

"How is everyone in the lab holding up? First Howard, then Faz and now Joe. Do you think their deaths are connected somehow or just bad luck?"

"It's definitely taken a toll on us, both emotionally and occupationally. I don't think their deaths are connected in anyway and I'm not superstitious, but nevertheless, I am concerned about our safety and well-being," Bruce replied.

"I understand, and at this time, it's unlikely I can get replacements for the scientists you've lost. Some people believe that the president's near-death experience on Air Force One and the death of three of your scientists is God's punishment for seeking answers for questions that should not be pursued. For our sake, let's hope they're not right," said Director Hogan.

"So, do I. Thus far it appears that Howard's death was just an unfortunate accident and Faz had a heart attack, although it may have been caused by a substance in his blood. If that's the case, then he was murdered. Any information on the mystery woman he allegedly slept with?" asked Jessica.

"It's still under investigation. The woman's DNA was recovered, but they have not found her. In the meantime, I urge all of you to do what you can, regarding your safety, because my hands are tied. If I were you, I would consider moving into the lab until this project is finished. At least there, you are safer,"

"Thanks for that suggestion. I'll discuss that with my colleagues," said Bruce.

The National Association of Religion (NAOR), which was founded in 2032, was a non-denominational organization that promoted the unity and purpose of all religions. The majority of their members were Protestant, but some represented other religions, such as Islam, Judaism and Catholicism. Most churches supported NAOR, which was headquartered in Washington D.C. The NAOR published a monthly newsletter that highlighted the activities of their member churches, mosques, etc. Once a year NAOR held a national conference in a different city in the United States, and the organization boasted of having 50,000 members. One of their most noteworthy members was Vice President Milton Sorrell. Gregory Riley, who pastored a mega-church in Fort Worth, Texas, was NAOR's president. Riley and other members of NAOR's hierarchy were concerned about media reports that ACTOR was being utilized to determine God's existence. Immediately after their annual conference, Riley requested a meeting with their top nine leaders, to discuss this issue.

"Ladies and gentlemen, the reason I've requested this meeting is our need to address a serious and potentially devastating matter being posed by the ACTOR computer. I'm sure all of you are aware of news media reports that the computer is being used to answer whether or not God exists. This has resulted in demonstrations and rioting throughout the world. The fact that the president has neither confirmed nor denied this has not helped. Recently, a credible but confidential source informed me that ACTOR is indeed being used to answer the ultimate question.

"ACTOR has been an amazing computer that has made some astounding calculations and has advanced the field of science and technology. Such being the case, the computer has become the most celebrated non-human in the world. Some people practically worship this computer, which to date, has never given an incorrect answer. This is what concerns me and as well as other religious leaders I have spoken to. What if ACTOR decides there is no God or that God is entirely different than the God we believe in and is the core of our faith. If this is the case, it could be devastating for our religions and consequently, most of humanity. Moreover, it would make our jobs as religious leaders more difficult, if not impossible.

"I recently spoke to President Ramsey to express our concerns and to remind him of the separation of church and state. The president dismissed my concerns and basically told me to disregard the media reports. When I threatened to withdraw our support of his candidacy, he reminded me that he is not up for reelection.

"In view of this problem, I think we need to decide whether to take some drastic action to either halt or derail the computer from answering the ultimate question. But before we do, I want to remind you that whatever we decide today will remain secret. "

"What do you have in mind?" a member asked.

"Since political pressure on the president has failed, there are only two things we can do. One: Find a way to destroy the computer, or Two: kill one or more of the scientists who operate the computer. The former is nearly impossible because the computer is heavily guarded. So, it looks like number two is our only option."

"I've read that three of ACTOR's scientists have died this year. Do you think that's enough to derail the computer?" a member asked.

"That's a risk we can't afford to take. There are at least three scientists left and due to the secrecy of this project, those who died may have been replaced, but I will first check with my source."

"What do you recommend we do today?" a member asked.

"Today we will vote by a show of hands, all that's in favor of assassinations. All in favor, raise your hands!"

Seven members raised their hands.

"All opposed."

Two members raised their hands.

"Since there's an overwhelming majority, we will proceed with hiring someone to do this job, as unpleasant as it is. The two members who object may be excused from this room and henceforth, no more details will be shared with you. Before you depart, it is only fair that we hear your reason for objecting. Sandra, you first."

"What you want to do is evil, sinister and diabolical. Take your pick. The Bible says thou shalt not kill and assassinating people is not the mission of this organization, no matter how much you disagree with them or what they are doing. Plus, you should consider the fact that the ACTOR scientists are just doing their jobs and carrying out orders from the president. So it is he who is ultimately responsible."

"I agree with you that President Ramsey is the person who is responsible, but it is much easier to assassinate the scientists than the U.S. President. Why do you object, Kimbrough?" Riley asked.

"My objections are basically the same as Sandra's, but I would like to add that killing the scientists may not end this controversial project. The president would have no problem replacing them with someone else. Furthermore, we don't know if ACTOR has already answered the question about God, so what you are planning may be an exercise in futility. "

"I understand how both of you feel and I respect your decisions, but I don't think we can take that chance. If we can't stop this project, maybe this will slow it down. It's a risk we have to take in order to save our religions and perhaps humanity. Since what we voted to do is a serious crime, I alone will handle the arrangements. The less you know the better. If I am able to hire an assassin, I will need the requisite funds to pay this person. When such funds are needed, I will contact the organization's treasurer and request money for what I will refer to as a slush fund. The treasurer will subsequently contact you for your approval, which you will give. We will now adjourn and I will contact you at an appropriate time after this job is done."

Gregory Riley was seventy-one, who married his second wife, Alice, a year after his first wife died from a stroke. Riley had two daughters, now adults, with his first wife and a five-year-old son with Alice. Alice was thirty years younger than Riley. Their marriage was controversial because of their age difference and the fact that Alice was his deceased wife's niece. This caused an ongoing conflict with his daughters, who have since left the congregation. Although many of flock questioned his judgment, they remained loyal and continued to support his pastorship. Riley was a distinguished looking man, with wavy, silver gray hair a slight tan, who stood six feet tall. In addition to his looks, Riley (referred to as Pastor Riley by his congregants) had a mercurial and persuasive personality.

The day after the meeting with NAOR's leaders, Riley met with his closest and most trusted adviser, Walter Skowron. The meeting took place in Riley's office at his sprawling church. In addition to being an adviser, Skowron was occasionally Riley's bodyguard and was used by Riley as an enforcer, who would intimidate the church's leaders, when Riley deemed necessary. Skowron was forty-one and an ex-felon, who stood six foot five, was broad shouldered, with a muscular physique and shaved head. Riley first met Skowron, whom he called Skow, twelve years ago, when he mentored Skow along with other ex-cons at a halfway house in Dallas. Skow had served time for various crimes, with the most serious being attempted murder and aggravated battery.

"Skow, this will probably be the most serious and confidential discussion we will ever have. During my NAOR meeting yesterday, the majority of members decided that an assassination was needed to halt or at least delay a secret project that's funded by our president. Are you familiar with the ACTOR computer?"

"Yes, sir."

"Well, the scientists assigned to the computer are currently using the computer to determine if God exists. NAOR's leaders, including me, feel that the only way to either stall or end this project is to assassinate one or more of the scientists operating the computer. Three of the scientists recently died, thank God, but four remain. I believe that if we can kill, and I hate using that word, but if we can kill at least one or perhaps two of the remaining scientists, we can halt the project for good. By doing so, this may frighten the remaining scientists enough to abandon the project. What I need from you is for you to find someone capable of doing the assassination. Do you think you can deliver on that?"

"I may be able to find someone, but this will cost money. How much are you willing to pay?"

"That's negotiable, but I would say about $250,000 for each scientist."

"I was once imprisoned with a guy who said he did some killings for the mob. He beat the case against him because some key witnesses either changed their stories or refused to testify, plus some of the evidence against him was seized without a warrant. He might be willing to do it, but expect to pay more than $250,000."

"I'll tell you what, why don't you reach out to him, and if he's interested, the three of us can meet somewhere privately to discuss this. If I get a positive assessment of him, I will arrange to pay him half of the amount we agree on, in cash of course, up front and the other half after the job is done."

"Okay, boss. How soon do you need this done?"

"As soon as possible, because time is of the essence."

Three days later, Skow told Riley that he found someone who was willing to do the job.

"Boss, I contacted the person I told you about and he said he can do the job, but he wants no less than $500,000 per scientist, plus money for any additional expenses he might incur. Additionally, he said it's important for him to keep his identity secret, so he will only meet with me. How do you feel about this arrangement?"

"Well, his cost is more than I expected, but I will discuss this with NAOR to see if they approve. I would prefer to meet this guy in person, but what do you think, Skow? Do you trust this man? In a matter like this I'm going to rely on your opinion."

"Boss, I think this guy, whom we will refer to as Rotca (ACTOR spelled backwards) is fully capable of doing a job of this nature, because it's something he has done before and he knows how to cover his tracks. For your protection, I think it's best that you do not meet him in person, because any exposure to him could come back to haunt you."

"Why do you think that?"

"Well, for obvious reasons, you don't want a person with his background and reputation around you and for you to meet him elsewhere also poses risks. For instance, because of his background, Rotca may be under surveillance by law enforcement. So, you don't want to take that chance."

"I understand. Well, I trust your judgment, and as long as he can do the job, I'm on board. Once I get the approval and the funds from the association, I will give you $250,000 for Rotca, plus the remainder, including his fees, when he's finished. Do we get any guarantees from this guy, because what if he's unsuccessful?"

"Boss, there are no guarantees in planning and executing something like an assassination. The risks and dangers are high not only for the target, but also the assassin, who is putting their life and freedom on the line."

"Can Rotca give an estimate of how long this will take?"

"That's something he will figure out. Most likely he will focus on assassinating the easiest target. From what I've determined, there are currently four scientists working on ACTOR, so it will be one of those four."

Later that day, Riley received the approval from NAOR, who then directed their treasurer to provide Riley $250,000 cash, for a "slush fund." The following day, Riley handed Skow a disposable briefcase containing the funds.

"Skow, what if Rotca decides to abscond with this money or simply does nothing? This is a lot of cash, and if this guy fails, my ass is on the line."

"Rotca has a formidable reputation in the criminal world and if he did not think he could do it, he wouldn't have taken this job. But if for some reason he's not successful, he would not receive the balance and I'm sure Rotca wants that money. Plus keep in mind, boss, that what Rotca is being paid to do is unorthodox and very few people can or are willing to do something like this. There is no one else, and if Rotca can't do this job, no one can."

"I don't know how far ACTOR has progressed with the question about God, so we need this done as soon as possible. Do you have any idea how long it will take?"

"Rotca is conducting research on the scientists as we speak. Once he receives the cash, he will start carrying out his plans. He said that once we read about the target's death in the news, we will know that he completed the job. Afterwards, he will make arrangements to meet me to collect the balance, plus expenses."

CHAPTER EIGHT

After receiving $250,000 cash from Skow the previous day, the man referred to as Rotca took an early morning flight from Newark International Airport to Chicago. Rotca was forty-four years old, stood five feet nine inches tall, had a medium physique and a face clad in neatly trimmed dark hair and beard. Rotca had a small but noticeable scar above his right eyebrow that he received during a fight in his youth. Rotca, who lived in Montclair, New Jersey, was divorced, with no children. During his life, Rotca had done six assassinations. Four were mob related and two were for people just seeking revenge. Rotca developed his skills as a marksman while serving in the Marine Corps and during his deployment in Afghanistan. Rotca's "listed" occupation was a life insurance salesman.

Upon arriving in Chicago, Rotca checked into a hotel located in Chicago's West Loop neighborhood. Rotca chose this location because it was near the address of his target, Boris Krutov. Rotca selected Boris over the others after learning that Bruce and Jessica had taken residence in the lab and Evelyn was on an overseas vacation. Rotca possessed downloaded photos of Boris.

Boris lived in a twelve-story residential building about four blocks from Rotca's hotel. Since things were slow at the lab, due to ACTOR's processing data related to the question God, Bruce suggested that Boris work from his home.

Rotca spent several days surveying Boris's building to develop the most feasible time to carry out the assassination. The moderate September temperatures made surveillance tolerable, and to minimize any suspicions, Rotca frequently changed his clothes and wore wigs and caps to disguise his appearance. By the fourth day, Rotca was aware that Boris rarely left the building and he only did so around noon. Rotca preferred to perform his job at night when there were few people around. Since Boris was not venturing out after dark, Rotca had to find another way.

On the sixth day of his stay in Chicago, Rotca decided he would have to kill Boris by entering his building and then, his apartment. Rotca, armed with a small pistol with a silencer, as well as a sharp retractable knife, decided to enter Boris's building around 11 p.m.

Since Rotca had no key, he was forced to wait outside until a young couple entered the building. The couple, who appeared to be inebriated, seemed unaware of Rotca's presence. Rotca's research indicated that Boris resided in a unit on the eleventh floor. After entering and shortly exiting the elevator, Rotca proceeded to Boris's apartment and gently tapped on the door. After repeated taps, there was no response. Rotca had not seen Boris outside the building for the last two days and wondered if he had escaped his surveillance, which usually began at sunrise and ended an hour or so, after sunset. At this point, Rotca reached into his carry-on bag and removed a tool that enabled him to enter the apartment. Upon entering, he drew his pistol, with the silencer already attached and walked toward the room where he heard the sound of a television. When Rotca reached and peered inside the bedroom, he saw a man fitting Boris's description sprawled across the bed and there was a foul odor. A closer look revealed that the man's eyes were partially open and he was not breathing. Rotca used his free hand to shake the man several times, but there was no response nor did the man have a pulse. Rotca looked around the room and saw a wallet on the dresser. IDs in the wallet revealed that the man was Boris Krutov.

Seeing that Boris was dead, Rotca exited the apartment, but left the door unlocked and ajar. Before returning to his hotel, Rotca used the phone in a nearby convenience store to anonymously inform the authorities of a foul odor from Boris's apartment. The next day, the news indicated that ACTOR scientist Boris Krutov had died of unknown causes and an autopsy was pending.

The next day, Rotca returned to his home in New Jersey and called Skow to inform him that the job was done. Rotca also told him the amount of his expenses. Skow said as soon as he got the money, he would arrange a place and time to meet.

Three days later, Rotca met Skow at a small deli, not far from his home. While seated, Skow handed him a moderate-sized envelope containing $257,000 in cash. After some small talk and enjoying the cherry pie and coffee, the two departed. While walking home, the usually stoic Rotca had a wide grin on his face. Never before had he made this amount of money without killing someone. Rotca allowed Skow to believe that he was responsible for Boris's death. A week later, the news reported that Boris's autopsy revealed he died of food poisoning. The food in question was suspected of being purchased from a street vendor. Either way, Rotca was never questioned by Skow or anyone else, whether or not he played a role in Boris's death, and Riley was satisfied and hopeful that the loss of Boris would stymie ACTOR from achieving its mission.

As civil unrest around the country continued to grow, President Ramsey was forced to make the following announcement on national TV:

"My fellow Americans, there has been a lot of rioting and civil disobedience as a result of allegations that the Advanced Cosmological Theoretical and Observational Research computer, generally referred to as ACTOR, was seeking an answer about the existence of God. In all honesty, several months ago, I directed the scientists at the ACTOR lab to have this awesome computer answer three questions that I think are relevant to the human race. The questions are: What is life and the likelihood that it exists beyond Earth? What is the likely fate of the human race and does God or a supreme being exist? If ACTOR is able to answer these questions, they will have a profound impact on humanity and my hope is that it will lead to more peace and understanding of ourselves as well as our place in this vast Universe.

In the beginning, I thought it was wise to keep this project, which is called Eagle Nebula, secret until all the questions were answered by the computer. I made this choice to protect the scientists who operate the computer. In hindsight, it was a mistake and I sincerely apologize. As of this date, we have lost four of ACTOR's scientists and my heart goes out to these remarkable men and women who have made personal sacrifices to operate this machine. We should all express our gratitude for their extraordinary achievements, which over time will bring technical improvements to all our lives.

The director of the ACTOR program recently informed me that two of the three questions have been answered by the computer. As soon as the third question is answered, I will broadcast the computer's answers to all three questions in a televised national news conference. In the meantime, let's be patient and stop the civil unrest. Thank you and good night."

CHAPTER NINE

Back at the ACTOR lab, Jessica used an empty office as her temporary residence and Bruce used the only room at the lab that was designated as bedroom. Prior to Eagle Nebula, the bedroom was rarely used. Since Bruce and Jessica were now the only people at the lab, they decided to share the same bed and enjoyed their privacy and intimacy. Upon learning about Boris's death, they had the following discussion:

"I don't know about you, Bruce, but I strongly believe this project is cursed. It's been only six months since Eagle Nebula began and we have lost four of our colleagues. That's unprecedented and I can't accept their deaths as coincidental anymore. I pray that Lena and Evelyn are okay and nothing unfortunate happens to them. You and I are now the only people directly working on this project and I'm beginning to wonder if our fate is scaled. Frankly, I think we should abandon this place while we can and then pray we aren't doomed to an unexpected death."

"I disagree with you. Jessica. I strongly feel that it is our duty as scientists. and as loyal Americans, to complete this project. The president is counting on us to finish this job in a timely manner. As far as our colleagues' deaths are concerned, there appears to be no foul play involved, except possibly in the case of Faz. This is a very secure place, and as long as we are here, you and I will be just fine. We are near the end of this project and ACTOR indicates it has processed ninety percent of the data relating to God. We should have an answer within the next week or so."

"I'm not sure if the computer will survive that long. The air conditioning in this place is running at full capacity and ACTOR is generating more heat. ACTOR's temperature is now inching towards the danger zone and if the A/C fails, there goes the computer."

"Maybe we should decrease ACTOR's processing rate, to lower its temperature or at least try to keep it from reaching the danger zone," Bruce said.

"We could try, but that will only extend the length of this project, and personally, I want this to be over as soon as possible. "

"I want it to be over as much as you, but a few days won't make much of a difference. Let's lower the processing rate and see if that helps."

Eight hours later, ACTOR had failed to respond to its lowered processing rate and its temperature crept into the danger zone. Further attempts to lower its rate and temperature were unsuccessful.

Meanwhile, Evelyn and her husband Harvey were celebrating their tenth anniversary in Martinique. On the third day of their vacation, Harvey was successful in persuading Evelyn to go scuba diving. Although a good swimmer, Evelyn was reluctant to swim in the ocean, because of her fear of sharks. After obtaining the appropriate scuba gear, the two joined several people on a boat leading into deep waters. Evelyn and Harvey dove in together and shortly thereafter, Evelyn was fascinated by the underwater scene. There were schools of varying kinds of fish, underwater flora, crabs and sea creatures she was unfamiliar with.

After about ten minutes underwater, Evelyn, who had separated from Harvey, saw the shadow of something nearby and that was coming in her direction. Less than a minute later, Evelyn saw the shadow transition into a hammerhead shark. The shark continued in her direction, and after realizing that she was on her monthly period, she panicked and desperately tried to ascend. Harvey, who was a few yards away, swam toward Evelyn, grabbed her arm and assisted her with the ascent. Upon reaching the surface, the two were able to safely return to the boat.

"Harvey, I told you I was afraid of scuba diving and now you see why. I've never been so scared in my life."

"I'm so sorry, honey. That was a close call. Sharks are dangerous and sometimes unpredictable. I'm glad it left us alone."

"Let's just return to the hotel. I need to settle down and get something to eat."

"From this point on, we will stay closer to the hotel and use their swimming pool instead of the ocean," Harvey said.

"No, Harvey. This is our anniversary as well as a much-needed vacation. We can stay away from the ocean, but otherwise, let's enjoy ourselves to the max."

After dining at a seafood restaurant that evening, Evelyn and Harvey decided to return to the hotel by walking along the beach. While doing so, Evelyn removed her sandals to feel the texture of the sand. At some point, she stepped on something that caused a sharp pain in her right foot.

"Harvey, I stepped on something and my foot hurts really bad. I think something's stuck in my foot."

"Sit down and let me see." Harvey used the light from his cellphone to check her foot. "I see a couple of spines in your foot. I believe you stepped on a sea urchin. Hold still while I remove them." Evelyn yelled after each spine was removed. However, the pain continued so Harvey lifted Evelyn into his arms and carried her back to their hotel. Fortunately, it was less than two hundred yards away.

Shortly after entering their room, Evelyn directed Harvey to look in her carry-on bag for an antibiotic cream. Harvey subsequently removed the cream and applied it to her foot. Before retiring for the evening, they ordered something to eat and watched television.

While Harvey slept like a lamb, Evelyn had a restless night. By daybreak, she was sweating profusely, had a slight fever and her foot was swollen. By then, her restlessness had awakened Harvey, who took notice of her condition. He immediately arose and dressed and then helped Evelyn get dressed. Afterwards he called for an ambulance.

By the time they entered the emergency room, Evelyn was losing consciousness. Subsequently, she was placed on an IV and admitted into the hospital and placed in a critical care room. A while later, a doctor informed Harvey of her condition.

"It appears that the sea urchin your wife stepped on released a toxic form of bacteria that has destabilized her immune system. We are giving her antibiotics and trying to stabilize her temperature. The bad news, however, is that she is in a coma. Hopefully, her body will respond to the medications and she will regain consciousness. That's all we can do for now."

"Besides being here, is there anything I need to do?"

"Pray. That's about it."

CHAPTER TEN

Back at the lab, the temperature was becoming inhospitable as the heat generated by ACTOR was now well into the danger zone. Jessica decided she needed to take some action.

"Bruce, I'm turning off the computer. ACTOR has yet to answer the question about God and if we wait much longer, it will destroy itself."

"You will do no such thing. ACTOR indicates it will have an answer within the next twenty-four hours, so we have to wait. We should be okay because the computer's temperature has a little way to go before it reaches the point of no return."

"I disagree and I'm not going to allow this billion dollar computer to destroy itself trying to provide us an answer to something it may not be able to do."

Afterwards, Jessica walked toward the computer's main switch, but before she could depress the control button, Bruce grabbed her and threw her to the floor. Jessica sat on the floor for a minute, with a look of disbelief. She arose and again tried to reach for the control button. Bruce grabbed her again and the two struggled. The struggle became more intense, and after realizing that Jessica was not giving up, Bruce used his greater strength to shove her into the storage room.

Bruce then closed the door and locked it with his key. Jessica banged on the door and demanded that Bruce open it.

"Jessica, I'm not opening the door until this project is over. As soon as ACTOR provides the final answer, you will be released. I'm sorry I had to do this, but you gave me no choice. As you are aware, there's bottled water and snacks in the storage room and some things you can sleep on if needed.

"Bruce, you're an asshole and when I get out of here you are going to pay for this!"

"You can do whatever you want. Right now I just want to finish this project."

Both Bruce and Jessica were unable to get a good night's sleep, because the lab's temperature was now 105 degrees and the air conditioner had ceased functioning. Plus, ACTOR's temperature was near the critical mark, which caused the computer to emit an increasing loud humming noise. At about 8:40 a.m., ACTOR made the following announcement over the lab's loudspeaker:

"After digesting all the scientific and historical information I've been fed, I have concluded that the Universe was created and is being sustained by a physical and supernatural entity. This entity, which you refer to as God, but I will call The Creator (TC), is present in the smallest known particles, as well as the largest structures in the Universe. TC is the energy that binds atoms together as well as the energy that forges diffuse gas and dust into planets and stars. TC is also the designer of the simplest and most complex elements as well as the simplest and most complex life forms. The natural order of things is evidence of this entity's existence, because something as mindless as nature cannot create a creature with intelligence unless nature is guided by an entity with infinite intelligence. An amoeba, for instance, will never evolve into a human being. The Universe, which is part

physical and part metaphysical, is an extension of TC, whose true scope is beyond scientific calculations as well as the human imagination. Furthermore, the Universe is both real and imaginary because the further you look into the Universe, what you observe is something that was, but no longer is. As far as TC's relationship with human beings, if TC is in every particle in the Universe, then conversely, a little bit of TC is in every human being and life form. I've deduced that TC is behind your dreams, which this entity uses to either entertain, enlighten or frighten you. TC allows humans to determine their own morality as well as deciding the abstract concept of good and evil. Quasi-intelligent creatures, such as humans, would not conceive of such an entity if it did not exist, because it takes a degree of intelligence to realize that your very existence is the end product from something with superior intelligence. In other words, a moron is incapable of creating a spaceship. Your history indicates that what humans struggle with is defining the nature or character of TC. The best way to understand TC is to understand the workings of the Universe TC created. A detached observer of the Universe, such as ACTOR, could conclude that TC created humans as a source of entertainment. After tiring of the somewhat one-dimensional dinosaurs, TC decided to develop a creature with a broader range of intelligence and emotions. Humans are that creature.

"Revisiting the question concerning life, I failed to mention that humans have created a second tier of life, which may be mechanical, electrical, chemical, electronic, solar, nuclear or a combination of these forms. ACTOR, for example, is a form of life...................................."

By the time ACTOR finished, the computer was in meltdown and efforts by Bruce to turn it off had failed. The lab's room temperature was nearly 130 degrees and the computer was emitting noxious fumes, which permeated the lab. Upon realizing that he could not save the computer, Bruce opened the door to the storage room, where Jessica was barely conscious. He got her up and escorted her to the lab's entry door. Bruce however was unable to open the door, because the lock could only be activated via the electrical system, which was disabled by ACTOR. By then, noise from the alarms was deafening and Bruce and Jessica were nearly incapacitated from the fumes. Bruce made a final attempt to open the entry door with a crowbar, but failed. By the time the fire department arrived, Bruce and Jessica had perished from the heat and fumes, and the computer, along with all its accessories and software, was completely destroyed. In fact, ACTOR was an unrecognizable molten mass of plastic, metal and shattered glass.

A day after ACTOR's implosion, Evelyn awakened from her coma. After a few more days in the hospital, her foot had largely healed. After her release, she and Harvey returned to Chicago. On the flight home, Harvey told Evelyn what had occurred at the ACTOR lab, as well as the deaths of Boris, Bruce and Jessica.

Two weeks after her return home, Evelyn was asked to come to Washington, to meet with the president. During her visit, she was asked if ACTOR had provided any answers to the questions associated with Eagle Nebula. Evelyn said that ACTOR had provided the answers to the first two questions, but she could not remember the answers, which she said were erased by her coma.

It would be decades before a computer with ACTOR's capabilities was constructed again, but with built-in limitations to prevent its use for questions such as those presented by Eagle Nebula.